THE TWO HUNDRED DOLLAR LOOK

F. E. PETERS

THE TWO HUNDRED DOLLAR LOOK

A NOVEL

LYLE STUART INC.   SECAUCUS, NJ

Published by Lyle Stuart, Inc.
120 Enterprise Ave., Secaucus, N.J. 07094
In Canada: Musson Book Company
a division of General Publishing Co. Limited
Don Mills, Ontario

Manufactured in the United States of America

Library of Congress Cataloging-in-Publication Data

Peters, F. E. (Frank E.)
   The two hundred dollar look.

   I. Title.   II. Title: 200 dollar look.
PS3566.E7552T8   1987   813′.54   87-1877
ISBN 0-8184-0434-5

THE TWO HUNDRED DOLLAR LOOK

Beginning

"You know, Catherine, you're not at all what you seem."

She slowly raised her eyes to the man sitting opposite her, his gaze stiff and bright, the wine glass slowly twisting in his hands.

"Am I better or worse, do you think?"

Worse he hoped, as bad as that other time, when the pain and the terrifying pleasure of her ran together and shook him where he knelt.

"Oh, better, much better," he smiled. "Some more wine, mate?"

She looked down again at her glass, which was still almost full.

"I don't think so. Not right now."

"Well, I can use a refill, I think."

He got up from the sofa beside her and went into the

kitchen. He opened the refrigerator and took out an unopened bottle of Pinot Noir from behind the chilled vodka.

I need some more tonic, he noticed. He wrote it down on a shopping list attached to the side of the refrigerator.

"What a lovely kitchen."

He glanced over his shoulder. She was standing smiling in the kitchen doorway, one hip resting comfortably against the jamb while her dark eyes ranged up and around the copper pots and pans suspended from the ceiling. He turned back to the bottle caught between his knees and pulled sharply at the corkscrew.

"I like to cook," he grunted. "Do you?"

She said nothing. She came up behind him as he bent over and thrust his own ten-inch slicing knife deep into his right kidney. He turned, his face amazed, and the bottle slid slowly, still intact, to the floor. A tiny trickle of blood appeared at the corner of his mouth as he crumpled forward, his eyes still on her, and came to rest at her feet.

She removed the knife, carefully washed it in the sink and replaced it in the wooden rack from which she had taken it. She dried her hands and walked around his body back into the living room. She put on her shoes, poured her undrunk wine into his potted spider plant and placed the glass in her purse. Then she let herself out of his apartment and caught a cab near Lincoln Center. It was done.

"Is that all?"

She lay on his couch in the office on Tenth Street, her eyes still fixed on the top of the tree outside his window.

"I said, is that all?"

"Yes," she repeated mechanically. "That's all."

"And why do you think you killed him, Catherine?"

"He was going to put his hands on me again, you know it."

"Did he give any sign? Did he say anything or do anything?"

10

She looked at the delicate network of blue veins that ran across the back of her long white hand.

"Why else would he have invited me to his apartment?"

The man in the dark three-piece suit shifted his weight in the armchair.

"If a man really invited you to go up to his apartment, do you think you would go?"

She slowly sat up on the couch and turned to face him. There was no sign of emotion on her face. Even her dark eyes, which she could never control, were dully unlit.

"Of course not. What do you think I am?"

"That doesn't matter. What do *you* think you are, Catherine?"

Her eyes dropped back to her lap and she said nothing.

It was not unusual, this silence between them. Silence had been his most effective instrument and her best defense all through their eight months together.

She picked up her handbag from the couch beside her.

"I think I'll go now," she said.

"Our time isn't up yet."

"It doesn't really matter, does it?"

She got up from the couch without looking at him again. She walked down the one flight of fire stairs to the lobby and out onto Tenth Street. A man turned to look at her as he passed. At the curb she briefly glanced up at Doctor Neil Astrakhan's office window, second floor front, and then opened her purse. Doctor Astrakhan was no longer watching, however. They had finished.

One

That was the ending, a curtain coming down on a pale sensual woman with long dark hair standing alone on the sidewalk of West Tenth Street. Earlier, not quite at the beginning, there had been another figure beside her, a young man of an easy and engaging manner, one Thomas Donovan, who served as a kind of *danseur noble* in his wife's improbably choreographed life. Put thus baldly, it does not seem like much of a role, that thankless and disinterested catching, supporting, steadying, but there were very few people who were inclined to question the arrangement once they got a little downwind of Catherine Donovan. Thomas Donovan was getting his all right, they figured, somewhere deep within those, will you look at them, thighs, smothered beneath those, just catch those will you, breasts.

Thomas Donovan knew better, however, and so he had rea-

12

son enough to question his self-effacing role from the beginning to the end of their brief marriage. And even without the training and experience of Neil Astrakhan, M.D., he could certainly hazard some crude conjectures. Thomas Donovan had of course his own sexual expectations regarding those same thighs and breasts, some of them ferociously vivid, others faint with despair. He never quite surrendered his expectations, however, even when a wiser and more realistic man would have long since thrown in his hand in disgust. The trouble was, Thomas Donovan was not a realist. He mistakenly fancied himself an altruist, a do-gooder without expectations. He was helping her, that's all. There is good reason why they call such dancers noble.

Altruism is a comfortable moral position almost immune to disappointment, and it was certainly useful to him in dealing with his wife. But it was also Thomas Donovan's livelihood. Monday through Friday he sat in a pale green office in a complex marked "Personnel," and in his easy and engaging manner he gave away livings to grateful petitioners for employment. Not very often these days, and not always to the people he would have preferred, but somebody at least took direct profit from Thomas Donovan's philanthropy on behalf of the New York Port Authority. He may have once thought in his altruistic way that he was giving his wife a kind of living too, but only until he had very recently discovered that she had a more than adequate life of her own.

The Port Authority personnel offices are located in a protected enclave inside and above a bus terminal seated on Eighth Avenue between Fortieth and Forty-first Streets in New York City. It is not one of New York's better neighborhoods, and the bus terminal itself is not a very wholesome place by anyone's standards. But that's where he worked, and so every weekday Thomas Donovan passed back and forth through the Port Authority Bus Terminal to his selfless calling. And every weekday at twelve-thirty he joined his fellow workers, some of whom he himself had hired, for lunch in the employees' cafeteria, where they discussed not their work but invariably the extraordinary setting in which they earned their daily bread.

"God, it's getting worse out there," Cindy Rehder intoned in the rising ritual mode to which her seniority entitled her.

Introibo ad altare Dei.

"Why don't they do something about it, like clean up that human garbage once in a while?" Thea responded as she delicately spooned a dripping glob of strawberry yogurt into her tired mouth. "There's a lot of room upstate for them."

"Like the CCC," Peggy said. Peggy was approaching a long-anticipated retirement, which gave her mind a practical cast. "Clean them up and put them to work."

"And those women, I can't believe it, what they do. And right in front of you."

There used to be more on that last topic, a lot more, but then Joan joined them a year ago and it was edited down. Joan was black.

"You ought to be glad Catherine doesn't work here."

That from Grace, and she took Tom Donovan a trifle by surprise. Grace was new to their company and didn't yet understand the unvarying sequence of clucks, sighs, antiphons and responses that governed this noontime liturgy in the cafeteria. As for Tom, he was somewhere else, back in the recent past, and not far from where they were then so cozily chatting. That morning on his way to work he had seen a black woman with blond hair, blond eyebrows and eyelashes, giving moistly gratifying oral sex to a gentleman in a business suit in the IND subway station on Forty-second Street.

He looked across the table at Grace, who was looking back shyly.

"I guess I am at that," he said.

Grace was pretty, he noticed again. He had recruited Grace three months ago. He called her into his office at four P.M. and told her she was hired. At four-thirty they left together, had a drink in a dark bar in the Port Authority terminal and went to her apartment on East Ninety-sixth Street and made love. He had said nothing about being married and she had not asked. Now three months later Grace knew his wife's name and was using it in public as if they were old girlfriends. Goodbye Gracie.

"And you know, it's getting worse." It was Thea again, attempting to pick up their frayed rhythm. "This morning there was a sailor exposing himself out there in the promenade. The U.S. Navy, for heaven's sake. I'm almost used to the creeps in the baggy pants and the raincoats, but a serviceman! I just don't know."

"And that guy is back on the subway station, the one who sells dope in the open," Vivian added. "I wouldn't be surprised if he was the one who pushed the girl, you know the one, in front of the train."

A chorus of clucks around the table to confirm this satisfying hypothesis.

The company was mixed at lunch but the men rarely clucked or even more rarely related to the ladies what they themselves had chanced to observe, often at very close quarters, going to and from work in the Port Authority building.

"There was a wino in the office the other day. He said he was looking for the men's room," Cindy began afresh.

"God only knows what he would have done there."

"I'd think he could pee in his pants just as easily in the promenade."

More clucks. And appreciative smiles too for the always amusing Cindy.

When Tom started working there five years ago he began counting the actual physical sex acts he had seen being performed in and around his place of employment. He used the strictest Defense Department criteria—mere possibles were not included in his tally—but even so he soon lost count, if not entirely his interest. Oral sex was an almost routine sight for him

15

now, but there was something about the gleam on that black girl's thighs that brought the early morning tableau back now at lunch. It was almost as if her legs had been oiled to a high sheen, he reflected as he munched on his roast-beef sandwich. And the sight of her curly metallic blond hair buried just below the vest line of an expensive blue pin-striped suit.

"Why are men such pigs?"

It was Grace's interpolated Amen to the luncheon liturgy. Goodbye, Gracie. *Adios chiquita.*

Missa est.

The Port Authority personnel department, managers, assistants, clerks and secretaries, gathered up the lunchtime debris.

"What's the matter, Tom? You looked unhappy all through lunch," Grace said next to his elbow as he collected his sandwich wrappings.

"Nothing much. I was thinking about you, as a matter of fact."

"Me?" she giggled sweetly. "What were you thinking about me?"

"I was thinking I'd like to have a drink with you one of these evenings. How does that sound to you?"

"Yes, Tom, a drink would be very nice. Just a drink, though."

"What else?" he smiled as he stuffed the sandwich wrapper into his coffee container. "After all, I am married. Thursday then?"

"Sure," she said.

Catherine was in the kitchen mincing vegetables when he got home that evening. He could hear the knife chopping away steadily on the wooden cutting board.

"Hi, I'm home."

"Hello," she said, her head still bent into her work.

He came up behind her as she stood at the counter. The

knife stopped. He gently parted her shiny black hair and kissed her neck. He pressed his hips up against her rear and nuzzled slightly between her buttocks. She stood there for three or four seconds, knife still poised in her hand, and then disengaged herself by moving to the sink and washing the knife and her hands.

He leaned against the counter where she had stood and watched her. Grace was prettier maybe, better featured and sparkling in a way that Catherine would never be. Men turned to look at Gracie whenever they glimpsed her passing smiling and excited through the open spaces on the sidewalk or standing bright and relaxed on the line in the cafeteria. But Catherine Donovan needed no spaces, no clearing to let the light get through. Men *sensed* her, felt her presence as strongly as an invisible and irresistible danger. At a party you simply approached Grace, drawn by an unreflective attraction, richer from the encounter even before it happened. But Catherine you instinctively scouted, measured, inspected, stalked in tighter and tighter circles, sniffing the air, testing the terrain. Grace was a cocktail, a little lust, a little fun, stir to warmth with a quip and a smile, swallow at a gulp. Good. Hit me again. Catherine Donovan was more like a potion concocted in some dark other place, ingredients unknown, dosage unindicated, effects inevitably interesting and just possibly fatal. Take, drink.

As he watched his wife he suddenly caught sight of the subway arcade again, heard and smelled the sound and odor of sex.

"Did you have a good day?" he asked. He picked up a raw carrot and put it down on the counter again. "It's Astrakhan day, isn't it?"

"Yes."

"How was it?"

"Tom, I'm not sure I want to go on with this analysis thing."

He pulled out the step-stool and sat down on it, carrot once again in hand.

She turned on the kitchen radio without looking at him.

17

The traffic situation on the FDR Drive was still not good. Amtrak and Metro North had half-hour delays. Subways and buses were all on time.

"Do subways really run on schedules?" she wanted to know.

"I think so. Yes, though don't ask me what they are."

"Who should I ask if I don't ask you?"

He got up, opened the refrigerator and peered inside.

"Want some wine?" he asked.

"You know I don't like wine."

"Well, then, how about a vodka gimlet with whipped cream?"

She continued washing her hands in the sink.

He took out the jug of Almaden Chablis, poured himself a glass and dropped in one ice cube, then another.

"Cheers," he toasted and drank. "So why do you think you don't want to see Doctor Astrakhan?" he asked. "You really haven't been at it very long, only a month or so."

She turned away from the sink at last and dried her hands. He watched her breasts rolling this way and that under the motion of her hands and arms. She leaned over and turned off the radio.

"I don't think he understands me."

"Maybe not, but there's not much chance that he will unless you talk to him. You don't tell me much, and I'm sure he's getting even less. Do you really empty your head in there?"

"I tell him all he needs to know."

"Terrific," he said. "we pay this bozo bags of money and you give him censored communiques. What do you talk about for forty-five minutes, the weather?"

"I tell him plenty," she said. "How personal do you think I can get? I'm not a whore."

Ah, the pity, he thought. The pity that Our Lady Star of the Sea in Bayside hadn't earlier taught a little whoring to the former Miss Catherine O'Rourke. Or didn't have an extension program for the present Mrs. Thomas Donovan.

"Well, keep trying," he said wearily. "I'm going to watch the news." He drained his wine. "Would you rather go to bed with me or Chuck Scarborough?"

"Tom, don't start. Please."

She turned back to the counter. She was wearing a white cotton dress and he could see the swelling and explicit curve of her buttocks where they pressed against the thin fabric. Catherine Donovan's body was only imperfectly confined by clothes. It smuggled out its unmistakable message around them or, like some rare and invisible strain of plutonium, simply seeped through them. It was never aimed, that lethal message; it struck the nearest careless bystander, who in this case happened to be her husband. He could feel a stirring in his own clothes.

He poured himself another glass of wine, went into the living room and sat down before the darkened TV screen. He was frightened. It didn't often get through, that fear he felt in the presence of the woman in the kitchen. It slept buried and restless under the cover of his desire. But he could feel it now.

Two

Tom Donovan met Catherine O'Rourke at the New School on Thirteenth Street in an evening class on photography. He had taken an architectural walking tour of lower New York and immediately decided he wanted to learn how to photograph those extraordinary buildings. Catherine had only a minimal interest in pictures. She was there because Maddy Kirsch told her she was twenty-six, which she knew, and that if she ever wanted to meet a man, which she sometimes did and more often didn't, she should do something about it, like registering for a course at the New School. Maddy Kirsch, who was already thirty, worked the East Side singles' bars in winter and cruised the Hamptons in summer, but she knew that Catherine O'Rourke was not up to that. So the New School. OK, Catherine thought she might after all like to take pictures of insects. Microphotography. Eckhhhh, said Maddy Kirsch, shaking her perfect blond curls.

Catherine sat in the corner of a back row, her preferred

place in every classroom she had entered since the age of six, and so Tom didn't notice her until they went into the hall for their first break. She stood with her shoulder to the wall, her eyes deep in a book. He saw the backs of her knees first, a part of the anatomy he had never noticed on anyone before, but hers were firm and taut and provocative. He passed by a little too closely and she looked up, not at him of course, but carefully into the open, empty spaces around him.

Catherine O'Rourke had long black shiny Sixties hair which fell upon her shoulders and guarded dark, almost black eyes set deep and strikingly in a pale face. He saw her mouth, a tight straight line, her uncolored lips welded together with a perfect seal. A saint's face, ascetic, austere, remote; a saint formed on self-denial, not on the softer stuff of charity. But unhappily for her, a saint betrayed by a body shaped, in spite of her will, for men's sin. Thomas Donovan remembered the first two thoughts he ever had about Catherine O'Rourke. Impossible. But how could anyone not *try* this one?

Thomas Donovan had come into his season for the impossible. Successes came easily to him, small-bore triumphs which he accepted with apparent relish and then put away in the drawer because their implication of failure offended him. Men liked him, women liked him a lot, and why not, he thought: he was an outgoing, attractive and intelligent single man who made few demands and rendered impeccable service. Not Servitude. Service. He was, as a matter of fact, all those things, but he was also easy, as his friends male and female knew very well, and as even he suspected. He took easy advantage, made small hazards and collected bronze medals, those shameful tokens reserved for the nice and the easy, runners without a kick. It was, if ever, his season for the impossible.

Catherine O'Rourke, one shoulder against the wall, her head shrouded in the disguise of reading, looked both incalculable and impossible to the easy and engaging and still unrealistic Thomas Donovan. A closed and locked room with "Do Not En-

21

ter" stenciled in red upon its gun-metal gray door. And though there was no public declaration of what was being so closely guarded, Tom understood as well as anyone else who passed that closed door the exact nature of the treasure within. It floated like phosphorescence off her swelling breasts. It gleamed from the white skin stretched taut behind her knee, from the sensual curve of her hip and thigh. It even glittered through the veil of her dark eyes which glanced up briefly to meet his own as he passed. It was, if Plato had ever looked at a woman, the very idea of *eros*.

The next week he made his first cautious approach in the corridor.

"Like a cigarette?"

"I don't smoke," she said with her eyes still intent upon the page.

"Chew?"

"What do you mean by that?" she said nervously as she finally consented to look up from her book.

"Well, sometimes people, when they're afraid to smoke, chew tobacco. You know, chew, like baseball players."

"That sounds very unattractive."

"Oh, you're right; it is. Because you have to spit every minute or so and it's very unsightly. But it relieves the nerves, I'm told.

"No thank you. My nerves are just fine."

He tried again the following week.

"Chew?"

She looked up. He held a stick of gum in his extended hand. The seal on her lips cracked a trifle at the corners. She took the gum.

"I'll have you smoking in no time," he said with a smile he had first tried on a nun in the seventh grade with astonishing success.

"I don't think so," she said. She unwrapped half the stick, put it in her mouth and returned the other half to him.

22

"What exactly do you want?" she asked as her jaws began slowly to masticate the gum into a pulp.

He looked at her. Her sexuality was almost palpable, he thought. It surrounded her like an aura. It came off her like incense in a still room.

"I don't know," he said at last, "but I'll think of something. Meanwhile maybe we should get to know each other before I start making impossible demands. My name is Thomas Donovan, and I know you're going to find this hard to believe, but I'm twenty-nine, straight and single. There, I told you you wouldn't believe it."

She had not in fact blinked an eye. But she was regarding him closely.

"You're married, aren't you?" she said.

"Cross my heart," he smiled. "You're single, aren't you?"

She did not appear to be greatly amused.

"Are you Catholic?" she wanted to know.

"Sure. Of course."

Let's not go too deeply into that, he thought.

"My name is Catherine O'Rourke. Class is starting again."

It took him another three weeks but she finally consented to have coffee with him after class in a shop on the corner of Sixth Avenue. Well, only half consented. The rest of the volition was supplied by Maddy Kirsch.

"You mean he's *single*?" Maddy said.

"So he claims."

"Believe him. Believe him, Catherine, even if it isn't true. Single *and* straight and alive in New York. It's like Santa Claus."

"Maddy, there is no Santa Claus. All he wants to do is have sex with me, I know."

Maddy Kirsch, for once in her thirty-odd years, was struck speechless.

"So you live on Seventy-ninth street. Can I come up and see you some time?" he inquired politely.

23

Tom knew that never, under any circumstances, would she consent to set foot across his dark threshhold on Charles Street.

"Why do you want to do that?" she inquired in return in a tone that suggested he had proposed flying nude to Caracas for the weekend.

"Catherine, you seem to live under constant threat. You're like your own Secret Service, checking out rooftops and buildings and rooms before you'll go in. You brushed off the seat before you sat down. You smelled the tea before you drank it. And you want to know the reason why for the most innocuous social requests. Who's after you? What do they want? Why are you in danger?"

She slowly stirred her tea.

"All right. You can come up and visit me sometime."

"And now you sound like a union negotiator who's been forced to make a work rules concession."

The seal on her lips cracked a little more. She drew her black hair across her mouth to conceal the damage.

"I'd like you to come up and see me," she amended. "Is that better?"

"And?" he prompted. "Come on. You can do it."

"I'd like to see you."

"Fantastic!"

Fantastic, if true.

She lived in a tiny apartment on the third floor of a brownstone just off Second Avenue. Kitchen, living room, bedroom concealed by an Indian print curtain. No TV. Books on insects and deserts and puzzles. A church calendar in the kitchen. A group portrait of the Sacred Heart, Saint Theresa of Lisieux and a third anonymous but doubtless extremely holy person on the dresser in the bedroom. No traces of family, of friends, of herself.

He bought his own wine.

"I'll bet you don't drink," he said.

"No, not very often."

24

"Well, if you have a glass you can pour me some of this."

She took the bottle into the kitchen and reappeared with two water glasses, one filled to the brim with wine for him, the other for herself with a damp puddle of the same at the bottom.

Well, she's trying, he encouraged himself.

"Cheers."

She must have gotten a little wine on her lips by mistake since she made a wry face.

He sat himself unbidden on the sofa, and only when he was settled did she sit in the armchair opposite and carefully tuck her legs up under her.

"Would you mind putting your feet on the floor?" he asked.

"Why?"

"I'd like to look at your legs, just to pass the time between questions."

She slowly extracted her legs and planted them on the floor.

"Would it hurt to cross them?"

She was about to say something, thought better of it, and crossed her legs.

They were, he reflected, very fine, long and full and firm, with deliciously curved calves and thighs that raced, as he would have himself, upward beneath her skirt.

"So," he said, trying desperately not to stare, "tell me about yourself."

She did, though not a great deal. Catherine could talk all right, if you permitted her, did not ask too many questions and did not stare at her body. He navigated the conditions very nicely, he thought.

Catherine grew up in Bayside, had gone to Baruch College and now worked as an assistant at the International Research Council where she answered the phone, wrote letters and kept track of globe-trotting professors. Tom was very interested in all the new details stitched on the portrait of Catherine O'Rourke, but he nevertheless took his leave exactly when he was supposed to and without having strayed from his assigned couch, except once when he raised his hand for permission to go to the bathroom and used the occasion to stealthily check out her bedroom.

"It was nice talking to you," she said as he was leaving.

"And?" he pressed.

"And I'd like to see you again."

Her mouth came all apart and she smiled.

Slowly he proceeded. Verbal seduction, always his strongest suit, got nowhere. Catherine would neither speak nor respond on subjects with the slightest sexual or erotic content, whether the material was cited from their own lives, the *Jesuit Relations*, Shakespeare or the Middle Kingdom of Egypt. Or even the sexual life of bugs, which he once desperately tried. Nor was there any visual or tactile suggestion from her side of the stadium. She had circumspectly crossed her legs for him, and continued to cross them without further request, and that was apparently enough. He got the sense of her body, but only with his eyes as she sat across from him or walked into the kitchen or came toward him down the street. And he certainly did not share his highly inflamed observations with her.

He did, however, get her to join him on the couch simply by asking her, though she stayed at the far end opposite to him and reburied her legs as a compensatory penance. Then finally, standing in the open apartment door before his departure, he placed a light kiss upon her lips. She seemed startled but she said nothing. On his next visit he kissed her when he came in, same chaste brush of flesh upon flesh. Again she said nothing, though by no stretch of even Thomas Donovan's flexible imagination did she return it. He took her hand on the couch. It was cold and tense.

"You know," he said, "you've come a long way. You didn't even ask me why I wanted to hold your hand."

Silence.

26

"And now that I have it," he continued, "I'm not sure why either. It's like a piece of ice."

"Tom, don't."

"Don't what, for God's sake?"

She got up and went into the kitchen.

When she returned he was waiting for her in the middle of the living room. He took her quickly, surprisingly, into his arms and put his lips full on hers. Her body went stiff, but he stayed firmly on her mouth. Slowly she melted. Her lips turned soft and her mouth gradually opened to receive him. He could feel the change of her body under his hands. It had been rigid at first, then softer, and finally and unexpectedly it came violently alive. She twisted one way, then the other, as if trying to tear away from him but clinging all the closer. He could not read her head, but there was no need: the entire struggle was being reenacted in the wildly writhing body in his arms.

"Catherine, come lie down with me."

"Tom, don't."

He took her by the hand and led her without resistance into the bedroom. She sat on the edge of the bed, eyes cast down. He put his hands on her shoulders and gently turned and eased her down onto the bed. He lay next to her and took her into his arms.

"Easy, Catherine, easy. It's all right. Nothing will happen."

She relaxed a little and he relaxed with her. She began to cry softly. He talked about baseball, about the Port Authority, about the cast-iron architecture in Soho, never removing his arms from around her shoulder and waist. He kissed her softly. She kissed him back, but more urgently. Her body began to move again, to writhe and twist slowly against his own in the bed. He kicked off his shoes. He reached down, unbuckled his trousers and kicked them and his shorts off to the bottom of the bed. Her hands never moved from his shoulders.

Her dress was already halfway up her hips. He put his hand beneath it and took hold of the top of her panties. She gave a sudden, violent start at his touch. Her hand went to her hips and then slowly withdrew, without a word. She neither helped nor hindered him, but soon he could feel her lower body pressed naked to his own. They lay that way for a while. He dared not do more for fear that he had taken her too far toward a place she didn't want to go.

She had not in fact gone with him. Catherine's body, which now began to rub against his own, was by now committed, perhaps determined, but her head had taken its leave to a distant land of dreams, of soft forests carpeted in dark green, of fields where silent brooks ran through a sunlit landscape. Her tossing became fierce and demanding, but with each thrust against her lover, each groan that escaped from her lips, her consciousness grew more and more remote from the desires of her flesh. He entered her, already slippery with passion, but she had long since gone to another place. Catherine O'Rourke was not present at her own deflowering, had no part in those explosive and endlessly repeated orgasms that shook her soft white body.

He sat on the edge of the bed and looked down at her in the half darkness. Her body was quiet at last, gleaming wet from waist to knees with their love, with one full, white leg draped protectively over the other. He knew she was not there, neither then nor before. He found her panties at the foot of the bed and carefully drew them back over her legs and hips. He slowly lowered her dress and smoothed her damp hair. And then, when he was finished, he dressed and went into the living room where he sat smoking and looking down Second Avenue until whenever she should choose to return and rejoin him.

"Did you have a good sleep?"

"Ummm," she stretched as she came into the living room. "What time is it getting to be?"

"Nearly six," he said. "it's getting light."

28

Her forehead puckered into a brief frown. Whatever thought had been there was quickly dismissed, obliterated.

"Catherine?"

"Yes?"

She looked at him sitting there with the dawn coming up through the window behind him. Her hand glided slowly toward her thighs, toward where he had been, then quickly withdrew, as if touched by fire.

"Are you all right?" he asked.

"I'm fine. But I think you should go. I'm sorry I fell asleep. I must have been very tired."

He rose to take his leave. He stopped before her in the living room, uncertain whether he should kiss her. Her hard-won equilibrium seemed so fragile that he hesitated to tip it out of control. Finally he kissed her lightly on her cold lips, murmured a quick "Goodbye," and left.

He called her the next evening but there was no answer. Nor did she appear at the New School for the next session. Then, after, three days, she called him.

"Tom?"

"Hello, Catherine. I've been trying to get hold of you. Are you Ok?"

"I'm fine. I just thought I'd stay with Maddy for a day or two. Tom, I got two tickets for a Mostly Mozart concert from the Council. Would you like to go?"

She was all right, he exhaled with relief. She had somehow, he didn't know how, come to terms.

"Great."

They both had, though he didn't realize his own terms at that moment. He saw her once or perhaps twice a week. They went to other concerts, movies, museums together. he sometimes held her hand and she sometimes took his arm. He returned from time to time at her invitation to her apartment on East Seventy-ninth street, but she was once again in the armchair, her legs tucked firmly beneath her. He dared not touch her or refer even in the most oblique way to what had passed between them. For her part, Catherine was less defensive with him, less guarded and nervous, but remote in some passive but final and convincing way. Something was over and something had begun. It was the best he could figure out under the circumstances.

After seven months of this chaste courtship he asked her to marry him. With only the slightest, almost imperceptible hesitation, she said yes.

Was there ever in history a groom who wondered if his wife would sleep with him after they were married?

Three

As a matter of fact, she didn't.

Well, once, after a fashion, three months after they were married, and it almost destroyed them.

They spent their honeymoon in the Virgin Islands, not without a little malign pleasure on the part of Thomas Donovan, particularly when he noticed that the now Catherine O'Rourke Donovan invariably called them "the Islands." But it was only a small pleasure and he didn't dwell on it for long. His pleasures were of another sort. He enjoyed their time alone together, not because his new bride was remarkably witty or intelligent or engaging, the way he was, but because she was filled with prospect and he with growing expectation. Thomas Donovan was like a grown-up child on Christmas eve, his gift still unopened in his hands, enough of the child to be filled with delight at the imagined pleasure to come, enough of the adult to postpone the revelation of the exact size and shape and quality of what had been given to him. So he took his joy in speculation, hefting the weight and mass of it, calculating its contours with eager eyes, unwilling almost to tear it from its richly promising wrapping.

He lay under the palms at Caneel Bay and watched his wife move slowly along the water's silvery edge. He thought she might bring with her some begrudgingly concealing swimsuit, but he need not have worried. She now stood on the fringe of the white sand staring down into the turquoise water apparently oblivious of the revelations that her black maillot sent rolling up and down the beach and most insistently to the man who was watching her from under the palms, his eyes half-closed against the sun. Her body was lavish to his sight, and she, with that sense she always seemed to possess, felt his gaze upon her. She turned, saw him looking at her, and quickly turned away.

At length she returned to where he was sitting in the shade.

"Catherine, love, you have gorgeous breasts."

It did not seem like such an immoderate thing to say, by a husband to his wife on their honeymoon, but she answered nothing, as she always did on that subject. No affirmation. No denial. No offering.

And that night she changed from dress to nightgown, as she would every night of their three years together, in the privacy of their locked bathroom.

Mr. and Mrs. Thomas Donovan had twin beds at Caneel Bay, as he had requested from the travel agent. He didn't want to push her. He preferred her to relax on her own terms. And he thought perhaps she did. She grew easier with him, rested her head on his shoulder or her hand on his knee, as they sat some-times back home in their new apartment on East Twenty-ninth Street. And the Sacred Heart made a miraculous disappearance. But he was permitted, and in the end took, few liberties with his new wife. If he put his hand upon her hip, he could feel her body tense. If he reached to touch her breast, she quickly turned away, not defiantly or even angrily, but unmistakably nonetheless.

32

But she was there waiting for him, he knew. When he kissed her full on the mouth, he could feel some echo of the vividly recalled twisting and writhing in his arms, the melting of her knees as if she would swoon. But when she felt herself getting too close to the edge, she pulled back, and he allowed her, without comment and without reproach. She was his; he could wait.

One Thursday afternoon Catherine spent her lunch hour in a bookstore on Third Avenue downstairs from the International Research Council. She slowly browsed the racks, taking this paperback or that in her hand, reading the back cover, opening the pages at random. She came to a halt. The book in her hands had no picture on the cover, no text on the back, but the matter within held her for a long time where she had paused. She looked again at the black cover of the book in her hand and then quickly at the young man behind the cash register at the door. She resumed browsing, pulled down a cookbook and a guide to the wildflowers of the eastern United States. And somewhere between the two she slid the first, black-covered paperback into her purse. She paid for the other two books and left.

When he got home from work Tom found her sitting reading in the armchair near the window. No, not reading. The book was open on her lap but Catherine's gaze was focused distantly out the window.

"Hi. Do you want to eat out tonight?" he asked.

She turned and looked at her husband. He had never seen that look before. He thought for an instant she might be ill, but when he knelt at the side of her chair, he sensed it was not that. Not that at all. The breathing.

"What are you reading, Catherine?"

"Just a novel."

She closed the book and placed it under her on the chair.

He bent and kissed the inside of her exposed knee. Immediately he could feel her hand pressing gently down on his head. He kissed his way slowly up the soft curve of her thigh and the

33

guiding pressure of her hand became more urgent. He could hear her breathing clearly now, could taste and feel the perspiration on her bare thigh, could smell some other smell. Quickly his head was between her legs, greedily feeding upon her. She held him there, held his head in her hands, dug her nails into his scalp. They slid to the floor together.

He was quickly in her and she was tossing and thrusting as wildly as she had that other time. But he did not grant her her body's wish. He slowed, then stopped, still thrust deep within her.

"Catherine."

Her eyes were closed, her head twisting from side to side, her face contorted into an expression close to pain.

"Catherine!"

It stopped. She began to return.

Catherine slowly opened her eyes. She saw him above her and her dark eyes grew wide with terror and fury. A fierce animal cry came forth from her lips as she grasped wildly at his face with her hands and nails. With a violent twist of her hips she thrust him out of her and over onto the floor. They sat there, neither looking at the other. At last he arose, adjusted his clothes and let himself out of the apartment without looking back to where his wife was sitting weeping in the middle of the living room floor.

When he returned, Catherine was sitting at the kitchen table, her long black hair pulled back, her head cradled sorrowfully in her hands. He sat down opposite her.

"Tom," she said shakily, "I'm sorry."

"It's all right, Catherine. It's all right. It just takes time. But you can't run away when we make love. You've got to stay with me. You want to, don't you?"

She said nothing, but he could see the growing tension in her shoulder and in her fingers as they grasped the loose ends of her hair.

34

Finally, she raised her eyes and looked at him. It was a look of the purest rage.

"You made me do it, you pig. You made me do it," each word as if chiselled in cold, hard granite.

"Catherine, we're married," he said as calmly as he could.

"It's filthy. You're filthy," she hissed back at him in spite.

His own anger was beginning to mount.

"It didn't seem so filthy or so terrible when you were doing it, did it? Or when you were reading that book. What exactly were you reading that made you so hot?"

"Don't talk to me in that filthy way. I don't care if you are my husband. Nobody can talk to me like that."

"Talk to you?" he exploded. "Don't you think that you talk too? Your body is always whispering its sexual message. Whispering? Shouting is more like it. I picked it up the first minute I saw you. Every man who comes near you does. You smell of sex. You stink of it."

"Tom, shut up before I kill you."

"You're a whore, Catherine. Pure and simple. A whore."

Tears were beginning to come into her eyes.

"And is that why you married me?" she asked in a suddenly quieter, sadder tone.

"In part yes," he said. He too was descending somewhat from his anger.

In part, yes; in large part, except that for all his expectations, he suspected from the beginning that he could never meet her price. What he hoped was that she would simply give him what he could never buy or extort or even take; that she might hand over to him out of charity the elusive gold medal she would never bestow from love.

"But I didn't marry you to practice celibacy," he continued. "You turn me on. Is that so bad? And worse, I turn you on. That's the worst of all, isn't it?"

She lowered her head into her arms on the table.

"I'm your husband, Catherine. I'd like you to kiss me. Is that a chaste enough love token for you?"

Silence from that dark head.

"You can't, can you? You can't even kiss your husband. Because if you do, you might want to do that filthy thing again."

"You made me do it," she moaned through the dense black veil of her hair.

A week passed, then two, and slowly they edged back to where they had been before his terrible miscalculation, to a guarded and measured affection spiced only with occasional glances and quick touches, in fun almost, and from him a sad and whispering sigh passed only in private on the street or in a bus or sitting behind his desk in the Port Authority terminal, where sex changed hands like the most common of currencies.

He lay in the darkness of Grace's bedroom and wondered how it came to be that he had slept more often with her than with his wife of nearly three years. He turned his face into the embroidered pillow.

"Tomas, what's the matter with you? Didn't you like it?"

"He turned back to her and took her in his arms.

"Yes, Gracie dear, I liked it. It was marvelous. It's always marvelous with you."

But never so marvelous as with Catherine O'Rourke that one night long ago on East Seventy-ninth Street. He still fed on the memory of it, still passed every night and every day with the now untouchable woman who had unconsciously given her body to him that night and then consciously and deliberately yielded nothing else for as long as they had been married. He had once thought of Catherine as a locked treasure-room. He always thought he knew what that treasure was, her sexuality, which he had once enjoyed. But it was not that which was under such close guard, he was beginning to think. Treasures are static, glittering but unmoving; what was inside Catherine Donovan was pitching and rolling, a hidden roiled sea, billows of lava whose heat and tossing he could feel even now in Grace's bed.

36

"I'll get us both a nice drink."

Grace got slowly and deliberately out of bed, turned on the light and let him feast his eyes on the body that had just been his.

"*Mira*, Tomas," she said, turning the inside of her thigh toward him. "It is running down my leg."

"Is that our drink?"

"If you like, my sweet man. Come, lick."

He did as she wished, but only because she wished. Like his wife, he too was incapable of giving himself to another at this moment.

He counted. Grace was the sixth woman he had had since his marriage to Catherine. The first time he was drunk, or nearly so, and went with Jack Charbonneau and some others from his office to a bar on Queens Boulevard. Her name was Carlie and he paid her thirty-five dollars to go with him into a sad room behind the bar and perform some act he could no longer quite remember. What he did remember was going home afterwards and staring, filled with cold sober guilt, at his wife across the kitchen table.

"Ok, Catherine, what's the matter?" he began even before he sat down.

"What do you mean?"

"Let's stop this nonsense, shall we? What's your problem with sex? Maybe if we talk about it we can work it out. We've been married eight months. I've tried not to press you, but we can't go on this way indefinitely."

"Thomas, I'm sorry. It's not your fault."

Her arms were clasped tightly across her chest.

"I know it's not my fault," he said. "It's not anybody's fault. But it's both our problem."

"Tom, I'm very tired. Can we talk about this some other time?"

"Like when? When we're fifty? Catherine, I'm not made of stone and I did not take a vow of chastity."

37

She got up without a word and left him sitting at the table.

It was, he later thought, his warning, delivered as directly as he could to a twenty-six-year-old woman who did not want to listen to or hear about or see or even think about anything that had to do with sex. Not a warning that he was leaving, but that celibacy, his at any rate, was not part of the marriage contract.

The second was Alice and he was not drunk this time; he knew precisely what he was doing. Alice worked in Schedules at the PA. She was an attractive, intelligent woman his own age. She knew he was married, sure, that he was courting her with no other intention than sleeping with her. She sized him up, weighed his pros and cons, the look in his eye and on his face, and said a smiling and gracious yes. It was terrific. Alice was terrific. And she was as easy as he was.

The third was a depressed little girl he picked up on the crosstown bus. She went to college and she was dirty. All over no less.

Grace returned with their drinks.

What's the point, he wondered. What's the point of being married when you can't sleep with your wife? What's the point of sleeping with people you don't love? And whenever he slept with these women, even Grace just now, he fantasized making love to his wife.

"What's so funny, Tomas?" Grace wanted to know.

Nothing was funny. His mind had drifted back to the arcade under the Port Authority, to seller and buyer of the goods he enjoyed for nothing.

"Grace, will you let me pay you for sleeping with you?"

"What's the matter with you? Are you *loco*? I'm no whore. I work for a living."

She slammed the drinks down on the table next to the bed.

"I was only kidding," he said.

"Well, I don't like that kind of kidding. If you want to give me a little present or something for the house, OK. But paying! Jesus."

38

"Look, Grace, I said I was kidding."

He leaned over and kissed her on her freshly glossed orange lips.

They made love again, against the grain of her anger, and again he thought of Catherine Donovan and the pleasures of her body.

Number four was a free-will offering, a woman he met at a party with Catherine. He scarcely remembered talking to her but the next day she called him at the PA and asked him if he was free for a drink after work. He liked the idea of a blind date, of tacking over to the bar of the Sheraton-Russell for a tête-à-tête with someone whose tête he could not remember. No wonder. She was not exceedingly attractive, was Gladys d'Ooge, but if anyone wanted it that bad, well . . . So they had two drinks in the bar and took a room upstairs, her treat, she insisted, since she enjoyed an expense account, and they had a perfectly wretched three hours, one of them attempting to have sex and the other two attempting to get the hell out of there.

And the fifth was Maddy Kirsch.

Four

"Tom, are you coming with us?" Jack Charbonneau called into his office.

It was four-thirty Friday afternoon, the witching and bitching hour for the male members of the PA Personnel management team. The ladies had their daily lunchtime liturgy; the gentlemen waited, like piously patient Muslims, for Friday afternoon.

"Where are we going?"

"Just up to the Rodeo. A couple of quick drinks and then home. No Queens Boulevard caper this time, I promise you."

Tom looked doubtful.

"Look," Jack said, all earnestness, "I wouldn't ordinarily press this, but it is Armenian Good Friday after all."

"In September?"

40

"You know the Armenian calendar," Jack shrugged. "Besides, why miss the chance; there might be an indulgence attached."

"What's an indulgence?" Tom asked with what he hoped looked like a puzzled frown.

"Up yours, Donovan. Your father used to peddle them in Astoria after he was defrocked."

"And your father got by, Jacques, but just barely, by peddling your mother's ass outside the shrine of Sainte Anne de Beaupré."

"Good," Charbonneau insisted, "we'll settle this at the Rodeo."

"Who else is coming?"

"Everybody. You, me and that gorgeous black tart who works the Nedick's down on the promenade."

"You're on," Tom said.

"God, if only I were," Jack sighed. "If only I were."

The black lady who had set up shop in Nedick's declined their kind invitation, needless to say—she was taking her Law Boards the following day, Charbonneau offered by way of explanation—but they went anyway, the men who hired the men who made the PA go, they hummed and whistled as they straggled up Eighth and across to Sixth Avenue.

"God, this is a long way," Gordie Lachlan complained.

"Think how long it would be if you lived in New Jersey," Charbonneau consoled him.

"I do live in New Jersey."

"See what I mean."

At five o'clock the Rodeo was already crowded, the best situated being those who had simply hung on at the bar since lunch.

"Greedy private sector employees," Charbonneau commented as he inspected the billowing mass of dark serge. "Can't even put in an honest day's work. Somebody call ICM and have these guys paged. The girls may stay, however, since it's Coptic Thanksgiving."

"I thought you said it was Armenian Good Friday," Tom protested mildly.

"That was bumped by the Puerto Rican Day parade, of course, with its usual privileged octave or alternate side of the street parking suspensions. Liturgy isn't your strong point, is it Donovan?"

"Christ, let's have a drink," Gordie Lachlan insisted.

"Boy!" Charbonneau summoned the young lady with very large breasts, mostly exposed, who worked, not entirely expertly, behind the bar. "Five vodkas on the rocks."

"I don't want vodka," Gordie complained.

"I was ordering for myself, wee Gordie. Place your own requests with the boy as you wish."

It was too late, of course. They all now stood with vodkas in hand.

"A votre santé," Charbonneau toasted, "et saint Pâques à tous."

"L'chei-im," a voice echoed from somewhere down the bar.

"Tasteless, just plain tasteless," Charbonneau commented as he disdainfully eased down his first vodka of the evening.

In the crush Tom's ascending elbow was jostled and came to rest under Gordie Lachlan's chin. The two of them stood drenched in vodka.

"God damn," Gordie whined.

"Suck it, man, suck it before it evaporates," Charbonneau urged him.

"Sorry about that," said a female voice behind Tom.

"Maddy! What are you doing here?"

"Same as you, Thomas, drinking in the weekend."

He turned back to introduce her. The PA delegation was now solidly impacted around the bar.

"Can I get you a replacement?" Maddy asked.

He looked down at his vodka-stained jacket.

"No," she laughed, "not another suit, another vodka. Jenny!"

The girl at the bar raised her head above the hunched revelers. Maddy made a "V" twice with her fingers and Jenny nodded.

"The perks of gender. Now all you have to do is go in there and get them. I'll be over there against the wall."

She took out a bill and stuffed it into his damp breast pocket.

"*Avanti*, my hero. And don't tarry with Jenny."

Vodkas in hand he found Maddy guarding two places at a table in a remote corner.

"What the hell was that racket at the bar?" she asked.

"That was Jack Charbonneau leading the CBS sales staff in 'Holy God We Praise Thy Name.' At least that's what it sounded like."

He put down the drinks and squeezed in beside her.

"Up yours," she toasted.

"And thine."

They drank in silence for a while, each uncertain how to handle this novel social situation.

"How's it going?" she asked.

"OK. How's it going by you?"

"Forget that crap, Tom. How's it going with you and Catherine?"

He looked at her sideways over his drink and tried to calculate the extent, and the truth, of his answer.

"Exactly how long have you been in this place, Maddy?"

"Since breakfast. It's the only way to get a seat."

She was licking the rim of the vodka glass.

"In that case I'll tell you since you'll remember none of it tomorrow. Not so good."

"I didn't think so. She looks terrible. While you, on the other hand, look terrific. Tom, you slinky bastard, you're not holding out on our Catherine are you?"

"And how's it going by you?" he asked.

"No, you're not holding out on Catherine." She squinted at him in the darkness. "You couldn't hold out on anybody, Tom baby, could you?"

He was aware of their knees rubbing together under the table.

"Maddy, behave."

"*Moi?* That's your knee, big boy. I left mine at the bar in the care of some creep from the legal department of Citicorp." She drained off her vodka.

"Do you want me to take you home?" he asked.

"Boy, *that* was *fast*, bimbo."

"Come on," he said. "You can come back for breakfast tomorrow."

He took her hand and led her out from behind the table, ran interference for her toward the door. She followed behind, one hand on his shoulder, the other administering encouraging pats on his behind.

"Tom, you'd make a terrific pulling guard. Did anyone ever tell you that?" she shouted over his shoulder.

"Not since the nun in grade school who told me I must never ever pull again."

She squeezed his shoulder.

"Me," she said, "I'm a tight end."

"I'll bet," he chuckled.

"True. Ask anybody."

He got a cab on Fifth Avenue.

"Same place?"

"Same place. Tom, would you ever give it up if it were yours?"

No, he assuredly would not. Maddy Kirsch lived in converted office space on the twentieth floor of the prow of the Flat-

44

iron Building where she bravely breasted the traffic flowing southward down upon her and which then eddied around her feet many storeys below. The only trouble was, you had to use the freight elevator after five P.M. and there was no garbage pickup.

"I hope the cretins on seventeen haven't frozen the elevator again."

They hadn't. It creaked down to them and then creaked up again to the twentieth floor.

They went in and he groped uncertainly along the wall for the light switch.

"Don't turn on the light, Tom. Come and look at this."

She led him to the curved bay window that looked far up Broadway and Fifth Avenue. The white headlights bore down on them like phosphorescent fish, parted below them, and then continued downstream as tiny red minnows.

They stood in the darkness and silently watched the flow of the traffic.

"Fuck Cleveland," she said and turned away.

"You've never been to Cleveland."

"All the better. Tom, come sit here a while. I promise I won't touch you. No, get us a drink first and then come and sit here.'

He found some vodka in the open kitchen and poured them drinks.

"Tom, you do know I got you for Catherine, don't you?"

"I've heard the story."

"Dumb bitch," she muttered.

"A little dumb at times, maybe; a bitch, no."

"Not her, you dumb fuck. Me. I should have kept you for myself."

"That wouldn't have been so good, Maddy. You'd make me screw all the time."

"Oho?"

"Come on, Maddy, you know all about it."

45

"Ummm. Tragic. What can I tell you," she shrugged.

"Do you know what happened to her? I'm guessing *something* must have happened to her."

"No, I don't know anything. Catherine is not exactly a big talker. What I do know is that she's afraid to put her finger up her own cunt. Metaphorically, of course. Uggh. Sometimes I'm disgusting."

Tom tried to imagine it. No, Catherine couldn't. Not metaphorically. Not any other way.

"Let's change the subject."

"A gentleman," she said, her head now resting back on the sofa. "A real gentleman. Want to go to bed, real gentleman?"

"That seems to be the inevitable conclusion," he said.

"Oh no you don't. Don't give me that inevitable crap. As old Larry Le Toole said to his Arab boyfriend, there's nothing *maktub, habibi.* If we're gonna do it, let's do it with a certain enthusiasm or else forget it. Got it, real gentleman?"

"You're right. Let's forget it."

"I didn't say that, wiseguy. If you're going to be literal minded, how am I going to be philosophical, huh?"

"Maddy, you got a big, fast sexy mouth. I think I'm going to enjoy this."

"That's a yes where I come from. Let's go, big boy."

She leaped unsteadily to her feet and tried to pull out the bed concealed in the sofa beneath them.

"I think you have to take the cushions off first," he said.

"All in due time. Don't be so anxious. And don't mind the sheets. They're a little dingy."

She fell onto the bed and began to struggle with her clothes.

"Be right with you," he said.

He went into the darkened kitchen and sat and had a cigarette. Two. He found a piece of paper and a pencil, opened the refrigerator and by its light wrote a note. He slipped back into the living room and left it on the pillow next to the head of the already deeply sleeping Maddy Kirsch.

The next morning precisely at eleven Thomas Donovan stepped off the elevator into Maddy's twentieth floor apartment with a small white box suspended from the index finger of his right hand.

"Good morning," he said cheerfully.

"Christ," she said, "I take it all back. You are a real gentleman. And you did come back. Are those the croissants?"

"Later. You smell very nice."

"I should," she grinned. "I've been sitting in a bubble bath for the last hour. And I even shaved my legs for you."

"So did I," he smiled back and kissed her for somewhat longer than either of them expected.

"Am I sober enough for you?" she asked when he finally released her.

"I don't know. Let's see you take apart the bed."

Maddy carefully removed the bolsters and cushions and revealed a snowy white bed within the couch.

"Catch the sheets," she said. "They still have the labels on them. Untouched by human bottoms."

They undressed in silence and lay down on the gleaming bed.

Suddenly she had both arms about his neck.

"Tom," she said softly into his hear. "Fuck me good. I need it."

"However you want, Maddy. However you want."

"Try this as a starter." Her mood was rising. She flipped over on her stomach. "Oh God, this is going to be swanky. Hit it, mister. *Hard!*"

Later she sat huddled in his arms munching on her croissant.

"Tom?"

"Um?"

47

"Get Catherine to a shrink."

"I've thought of it."

"Well, do it. Look, I don't mind borrowing a little of what she's not using, but I could get terribly used to this. Terribly. Any guy who refuses to screw a drunk broad and then shows up the next morning with croissants and screws her sober, he can own me. And I mean *own*."

She took another bite.

"Tom?"

"Um?"

She turned in his arms and was now looking up at him.

"Why aren't you miserable? Another guy would have cut out on her long ago. But you, you hang in there and you don't even seem terribly unhappy. I assume you're getting some on the side—shshsh, don't say anything—but that's not the point. How do you stand it, the neurosis, the sex psychosis, whatever it is Catherine's caught up in?"

"I have to, Maddy."

"Have to? Have to what, for Christ's sake?"

"To help her, I guess. You know, when I first met Catherine, she struck me as a little shaky, as if you had to be gentle with her or she'd topple over. Precarious. I'm sure I was right; she was precarious. But she wasn't about to topple over. She had managed to get herself into some kind of equilibrium, wobbly maybe, but some kind of equilibrium. Then I came along and either she misjudged or I misjudged that she could walk the same tightrope with another person on her shoulders. She did, for a while, but she's beginning to shake now; the balance is going. I did it, I know, and I've got to try to help her."

Maddy shuddered in his embrace.

"Tom, don't be a fool. Get her a shrink, please. I don't have the slightest idea of what's screwing up Catherine and neither do you." She leaned up and planted a kiss on his lips. "Maybe she just doesn't like you."

"Come *on*," he smiled.

"No, I didn't think that would appeal to you. Anyway, the point is, if *you* start fooling around with her head, you're only going to make it worse, a lot worse."

"I guess you're right. I don't know what's going on inside Catherine. I can hear it, but I don't know what it is." He rested his chin on the top of Maddy's curly head. "But what do I know from psychiatrists?"

She turned and pulled away from him.

"Tom, you innocent, for once you've fallen into the right bed."

"Do you know any?"

"Only a thousand or so," she said. "I have a whole book of them."

She scrambled up naked from the bed and ran on tip-toe over to her desk. She returned flourishing a small black book with a skull and crossbones stamped in gold on the cover.

"OK, let's do this scientifically," she said, settling herself back onto the bed. "I'll close my eyes, flip the pages and pick one at random."

"That's crazy," he said, laughing.

"So what do you think this is all about, you dummy. One, two . . . " Her finger twirled in the air. "Three. Bingo! Who did I pick?"

He looked where she was pointing.

"Mario Schnorr."

"My God!" she howled and fell back on the bed.

"Who is he? Do you know him?"

"Know him?" she screamed again as she kicked her bare legs toward the ceiling. "He's my ex-husband."

"Maddy, I didn't know you were married."

"Oh goodie, then my hymen must still be intact. Of course I was married. You don't think I'd be farting around singles bars at thirty-three, do you, if I'd never been married?"

"What difference does that make?"

"Principle, Tom, the all-important principle. Nobody who's

49

really single ever goes to a singles bar. Let's try again. I can't send her to Mario."

She took up the book again.

"One, two, three, boom!"

"Sylvan Busch, M.D.," Tom read off from under her finger.

"Christ, that fag died years ago. I've really got to work on this book. OK, this is it. Third time is lucky time. This is a definite. Three, two, one aaaaandd fuck *you*. Who?"

"Neil Astrakhan."

"Who the hell is he?" she demanded. "Here, let me see."

She snatched the book from his hands.

"Tenth Street. Damn strange, I never heard of him."

"It's in your writing," Tom said.

"Yes, I wrote it. Jesus. I wonder. Could it be I slept with him during the blackout?"

"Maddy, this really doesn't seem like a very good idea to me."

"Tom," she insisted, "you really don't know anything about this. Do you know, by any chance, how many shrinks there are in New York?"

"A lot," he conceded.

"A whole lot. And there's no reason, not the slightest, why you should choose one over the other. It's not like a brain surgeon where you can find out how many people he's killed and how many he's cured. But shrinks, who knows, so why not go the I Ching way? There ain't a hell of a lot else to go on."

"So why go to one, then?"

"Because they're all kind of cute fellahs," she smiled as she ran her finger over his lips, "some of them with beards. And it's also nice to have someone to talk to, even at those stiff rates, and God knows Catherine needs that." Her brow became knitted up. "Who the hell *did* I sleep with during the blackout? What a thing to forget."

Five

Tom dialed from the middle of the rumpled white bed far above the eddying currents of Fifth Avenue and Broadway.

"Hello, Mr. Astrakhan?"

Maddy rolled her eyes toward the ceiling.

"Doctor Astrakhan," the voice on the other end of the line insisted, with a small tasselated fringe of annoyance around its edge.

"Doctor Astrakhan. Sorry," Tom corrected. "This is Thomas Donovan. I've been recommended to you by Maddy Kirsch."

"Who?" the voice wanted to know.

"Maddy Kirsch."

A brief memory search at the other end.

"Tell him I'm a woman," Maddy hissed. "Sometimes people get confused."

"It's a woman," Tom added.

"I'm afraid I don't know any Maddy Kirsch."

Tom shook his head at Maddy.

"Well, it was a blackout after all," Maddy sulked. She went over and inspected her still unclothed body in a mirror on the wall.

"She's the wife of Mario Schnorr," Tom continued a little desperately.

"Who?"

"Mario Schnorr."

Further search. Tom shrugged across the room to Maddy who was now briskly massaging her breasts in front of the mirror. She shrugged back.

"I'm afraid I don't know him either. Look, Mr. Donahue. I'm really extremely busy at the moment."

"Donovan. Yes, well, it doesn't have anything to do with either of them. I'm really calling about my wife. I think she needs some assistance. You know, help."

He heard himself sounding like a fool.

"Why isn't she calling then?" the voice asked.

"Well, I haven't spoken to her yet."

"Tell him to go fuck himself," Maddy called in from the kitchen where she was making lunch.

"Well, then, Mr. Donovan, I suggest you do. And then have *her* call me."

"Yes, I see."

"Good. Goodbye, Mr. Donovan."

Tom sat and looked glumly at the telephone on the bed.

"I wish I hadn't done that," he said.

"Shrinks always make you feel that way," Maddy said cheerfully as she placed down on the bed two bagel and cream cheese sandwiches on paper plates. There was a cauliflower garnish on each.

"I'm on a cauliflower diet," she explained.

"Why are women always on diets?"

"Because," she smiled, "we're all afraid that our big, brave, handsome men will think we're fat."

"I don't think you're fat. Can we throw away the cauliflower?"

"Sure, sweets."

She removed the piece of raw cauliflower from each place and thrust them under the pillow on the bed.

He looked at Maddy over his bagel sandwich. Her body looked like Catherine's with all the options removed, he thought. No fog-lights, chrome trim, racing mirror, wire wheels, sun roof or luggage rack. Just a functional chassis, lithe and lean and trim.

"Thinking of buying?" she finally asked.

No, he preferred all the optional extras, but the Maddy Kirsch model sure handled terrific on the curves. Acrobatic Maddy was. Just plain acrobatic. He could still feel the ache in his hip joints.

"You're very acrobatic," Tom said.

"You're very attractive yourself," she pouted.

"Don't fish," Tom said. "You know you're attractive. Half the women in New York would sell their souls for your hair."

Maddy Kirsch's face was surrounded by a halo, an aura of blond curls, each perfectly sculpted even now, and each the color of natural golden corn. It was a place to get lost, to settle into and sleep a deep golden sleep.

She licked the cream cheese from around the edge of her bagel.

"You know," she said, "I wasn't really married to Mario. I just lived with him for a couple of years."

Tom said nothing. That must have been difficult, he thought, that apparently casual confession.

"He was a fool," Tom said at last when she did not break the silence.

"Oh, I don't know. I kept a nice house."

"You know what I mean, Maddy."

"You're not only pretty, Thomas; you're also sweet. Come kiss me."

He leaned over to kiss her and found instead a finger covered with cream cheese thrust deep into his mouth.

"Now kiss me," she smiled.

He did, right through the smile and the cream cheese.

"Can we talk about Catherine a minute?" he asked.

She fetched up a deep mock sigh.

"OK. Shall I put on my panties for this?"

"You remember," he said, "before we were married, Catherine stayed over with you a couple of days. Do you remember that?"

Maddy sat chewing thoughtfully on her knuckle.

"Do you know what happened then? We had sex for the first time. Did she tell you?"

She shrugged and addressed her attention to her toes.

"Maddy, don't you want to talk about this?"

"I guess not," she said. "We all have different versions of reality, all of us, and it sometimes doesn't seem fair to have your friends sit down and catch you in the same lies we all tell ourselves. What does it prove?"

"Nothing, I suppose."

"Tom." She crawled over to him, pushed him back on the bed and looked down into his face, her two arms straddling his shoulders. "Tom, divorce her."

"Why?"

"For her sake, not yours or mine. I've been thinking about what you said before about destroying her equilibrium. I think you're right, but maybe not for the same reason. Catherine's no basket case. She got through school, had a good job and took care of herself perfectly well before she met you. She had it together, sort of, at least as well as any of us has it together. OK, she had problems with men, but what else is new? What you did, my man, was put sexual pressure on her. You caught her unawares or stupid or drunk—no, not drunk—but something, and you made her open the little box she had nailed shut. Not nice. But what's worse, now you're hanging around with a license in your hand saying you can even do it again, and any time you choose."

"So why did she marry me?"

"Who knows? Maybe she loves you. Why don't you ask her?"

He looked at her in silence. She descended to him and rested her golden locks next to his head.

"Thomas," she said after a while, "let's make love again. No acrobatics this time. Just tender love."

"Like lighting a candle," he said.

"Like lighting a candle," she agreed.

There are not as many candles as there used to be in New York City. Between them the Fire Code and Vatican II seem to have snuffed most of them out, but there are still some around, if you know where to look. Saint Agnes Church on East Forty-third Street still has them, for example, guttering quietly, tenderly, with the hopes of the faithful.

Catherine knew what the sign on the confessional said; she had been studying it in the candlelight of Saint Agnes's for weeks as she knelt beneath the dark pillars. It was a notice of vacation of premises, a warning that the business was failing. "Confessions in Rectory. Sat. 4-6 P.M."

When Catherine first saw it her heart trembled. She had forced herself into the church, forced herself to the point of performing a childhood exercise that now provoked only fear and anger. She was accustomed, from the long past, to enter the dark and anonymous confessional where she would, in the end, press her nails painfully into her flesh and constrain herself to kneel and beg forgiveness from a man. And now, she was told, she was being deprived of that saving anonymity. If she wanted the balm, she would have to mount the stone steps of

Gaudaloupe on her knees, face whatever censorious woman answered the rectory bell, petition audience, throw herself naked before the priest and beg indulgence.

It was a young man who answered the doorbell. He was wearing running shoes, she noticed immediately. You used to be able to identify them by their shoes, she thought. The world had moved on.

"I want to go to confession."

The young man nodded and pointed to a room off the entry hall.

"Will you wait in there please. Father will be with you in a minute."

She went in and a bell sounded somewhere inside the house. The last parlors in the world, she thought. She remembered once trying to reach a rabbi for the Council. When she called the synagogue his secretary answered, "Rabbi Holtzman's study." Did they pick up the phone here and say, "Father Flanagan's parlor. May I help you?" She stood before what seemed to be a confessional, just a small portable screen with a kneeler on one side and, yes, a chair on the other.

A door opened somewhere behind the screen and somebody settled into the chair. She could imagine him draping the thin purple stole around his neck. She knelt on the wooden kneeler.

"Bless me, Father . . ."

"Do you want simply to confess or do you want to talk?" a voice interrupted from the other side of the screen.

She wanted to run. To kick over the screen and strike out with her fists at the man sitting on the other side.

"Talk."

"Fine."

He emerged from behind the screen, stole in hand, a gray man in his late fifties with shiny black pants and a denim shirt. And black shoes. He motioned her to two armchairs drawn up just the right distance apart under a large and stern color portrait of the Cardinal Archbishop of New York.

They settled themselves. He took his cigarettes out of his shirt pocket.

"Care for a cigarette?" he asked.

"I don't smoke."

"Do you mind if I do?"

"Yes. I'd prefer you didn't. I'm allergic."

He put his cigarettes and lighter with his stole on the table beside him.

"This is not always easy," he began. "Though it's a lot easier for me than for you, I confess." He smiled at his small professional joke. "So relax and take your time. I know people don't come in here just to say 'hello.' They come because they're troubled. It's a state we all share together. Nobody has cornered the market."

At least he didn't say "my child," she thought.

"So begin wherever you wish," he invited.

"I'm married."

She wanted desperately to leave.

"And my husband . . . he . . ."

"How long have you been married? Do you mind if I help with some questions?"

"Two and a half years."

"Is he a Catholic?"

"Yes. Can I get a divorce?"

"Why do you want a divorce?"

Catherine sat looking at his cigarettes. Why had she said she wanted a divorce?

"I really don't mind if you smoke," she said.

"It's all right," he said. "I can survive."

"No. Please, go ahead."

He lit one of his cigarettes.

"Are you sure you won't have one?" he asked.

She reached out and took one of his cigarettes, put it to her lips, and he bent over and lit it. She took it from her mouth and looked at it curiously. It was the first cigarette she had ever smoked in her life.

"Why do you want a divorce?" he resumed.

"I don't want a divorce. I love my husband. I want to live with him. But I can't, well, I can't sleep with him. You know what I mean."

"Why not? Why can't you sleep with him? There's nothing wrong with sex."

She grimly smiled her silent rebuttal at him and he smiled back his gracious concession of defeat.

"Well, almost nothing wrong with it," he amended. "Have you ever slept with him?"

"I'm not sure."

He sat studying the woman next to him. Catherine's legs were crossed and the toe of her foot pointing toward him now was twitching rhythmically and violently to and fro.

"I see," he said.

"No you don't," she almost shouted at him. She threw the cigarette into the ashtray. "The sin is not mine. The sin is the Church's for demanding that I do something I don't want to. I hate it. It's filthy and disgusting and you sit there and tell me I have to do it because I'm married. What has it got to do with love? With anything?"

Her last words came out in gasps, as if she was starving for air. She sat slumped in her chair, the cigarette smouldering unquenched in the ashtray at her side.

"You have no sin," he said gently when he was sure she had finished.

She looked up again, her eyes still bright.

"Then what am I doing here crawling in front of you? Why have I been sitting crying in your ugly church for weeks? Why? Tell me."

"You have guilt maybe, but no sin."

He put out his hand to touch hers but she recoiled as soon as she saw what he was about to do.

"Don't touch me," she said in a tone filled with menace.

"I'm sorry," he said. "I didn't intend anything."

Catherine suddenly became quiet, almost demure. She looked at him and smiled.

"Oh, didn't you?" she murmured. "You seem like a very understanding man." She began to unbutton her blouse. "Are you also a holy man? Come, tell me."

"Don't," he said quietly.

Her blouse was now unbuttoned. She unhooked her bra at the front.

"We're all troubled, Father. What are your troubles? Do they look like these?"

She sat before him holding her blouse and bra apart to reveal her full breasts, her erect nipples.

"Look but no touch, Father. Just something to think about later."

He picked up his cigarettes and his stole. His eyes were on her face.

"I don't think I can help you," he said rising. "But you came here after all and maybe that's enough. I'm very sorry. I'm only a priest."

He turned and left the room.

Still smiling, Catherine refastened her bra and buttoned her blouse. She picked up the cigarette from the ashtray and walked over to the parlor window. Her left hand was on her thigh. She stood there stroking her own flesh, looking out at the passers-by on Forty-third Street.

Six

Catherine worked at a "station" outside her boss's office at the International Research Council. Not a very elegant name for a workplace, granted, but not entirely inappropriate either, since Catherine Donovan unmistakably took her personal stand in that space. It was hers and hers alone, and woe quickly befell anyone, secretary, program officer or president, who cast hands or eyes upon her desk, intruded into its folders and drawers, onto its public plateau or into its private canyons. Her desktop was arranged for her needs and her very private desires. She borrowed nothing. She loaned nothing. Her pencils were sharpened and her papers neatly stacked. And Thomas Donovan smiled his approval over this orderly landscape from out of a sterling silver frame which she had deposed next to the Council directory.

Her boss's name was Gillespie. He was a program officer of the Council and he handled the complicated affairs of the Slavic

60

peoples. Down the hall Mr. Coulson dealt with the tumultuous
Latin Americans and Mr. Unser with Africa, while around the
corner and happily out of sight Mr. Hopper tried to cope with
the troublesome Middle East. Each had his own Catherine, but
Mr. Gillespie's was the original, as he often told his colleagues in
private over drinks in the Council library. No argument there.
Mr. Hopper, for one, was in absolute awe. "My God, what an
ass," he was often heard murmuring into his Beefeater martini.
"Like a perfect Sahara dune." Mr. Hopper had never been near
the Sahara, or anywhere, of course, near that quite perfect dune
just down the hall.

Mr. Gillespie had a different perspective. He could sit at
his desk all through the day and observe Catherine Donovan
through his doorway in undisturbed, even subsidized tranquil-
lity. Walking way from him down the hall, hips rolling. Bending
her blinding thighs or breasts over the files. Sitting with her
back to him in the secretarial chair that so lovingly embraced
and freeze-framed her hips and buttocks for his leisurely contemplation.

But Mr. Gillespie was not exactly envied his good fortune.
He was a rather proper man, careful in his propensities and de-
voted, it was said, to his equally proper family in Rye. And second, and finally, Catherine Donovan had firmly declared herself, like her desk, decisively off-limits, and everyone had an
exact comprehension of how tough a cookie Catherine Donovan
was. "She pitches nothing but strikes," the awed Mr. Hopper
had once remarked to Mr. Coulson, and there the consensus
rested. Nothing but strikes and nothing but fastballs.

Catherine knew all about it. She could sense a male stare
around a corner, through a brick wall, and the hairs on the nape
of her neck stood up on end at the merest hint of an untoward
glance. She got more of them than she knew, however, since she
had reduced her admirers to furtive glances and veiled stares,
and only when they were sure she was not watching.

The Council officers she had pretty much under control,

she knew. Where the trouble more often arose was from the academics who were constantly drifting into 605 Third Avenue to report on their fortunes or beg for new ones. They came in search of travel grants, publication subsidies, a pile of green just large enough to support an international conference; what they found instead was far more enlarging, Catherine Donovan. They gawked, then smiled, made indelicate little suggestions on the foolish premise that the professorial charm that had knocked three hundred coeds dead in Bloomington or Buffalo or Bowling Green would work its same magic on Catherine Donovan. But not for long. Quickly the message came rolling down like thunder from Sinai, and even the daffiest Assistant Professor of Czech either ducked or got off the slopes. Or had his grant application or boondoggle permit inexplicably lost. Only strikes and only fastballs, as Mr. Hopper had sagely observed, but Catherine Donovan could also throw at your head if you leaned too far out over the plate.

She did permit one little indulgence, however. She occasionally permitted Mr. Gillespie to take her to lunch. They strolled over to Le Petit Canard on Second Avenue, had a perfectly proper, unalcoholic lunch and strolled back to the Council where everyone spent the rest of the afternoon wondering why poor Gillespie took the trouble to try to climb Everest in his bare feet. They wondered for their own amusement, of course. Not with that bimbo, they knew. Never.

Thomas Donovan naturally assumed almost epic proportions at the International Research Council. He had scaled that treacherously frozen peak, had clambered up and over that perfect dune. Catherine Donovan went home, they whistled to themselves, and climbed into bed with someone named Thomas Donovan who then screwed the stuffing out of her. Wow. Tom showed up at the Council offices in the flesh on occasion, and when he did he was followed down the halls with almost as many stares as were collected by his wife on her own voyages across the carpet. How did he do it, the men wondered. Cute, the

62

women thought, but how does he stand her—particularly the unhappy females who had messed with Catherine Donovan's virginal desk.

Then there was that bright Monday morning, not unlike the one in Sarajevo when the First World War exploded and destroyed the old ways forever. Catherine Donovan sat down at her desk, a trifle late this historic Monday, took a porcelain ashtray from her handbag, and lit a cigarette. All the heads on the row of stations turned ever so slightly to observe the wonder. Mr. Hopper observed it too, one hand frozen on his fly en route to the men's room. Well, I'll be piss damned, he thought.

Indeed he would.

Catherine sat with the cigarette poised awkwardly in her hand and thought of the scene in the St. Agnes Rectory. She had played it over and over again in her mind Saturday night and all day Sunday. She did not picture herself in that *tableau vivant*, however. She was always behind the camera watching the priest and experiencing the emotion of it. Odd, she thought as she now sat at her desk at the Council, she was not embarrassed. She saw herself not as she was but as she was reflected in the priest's startled and discomfited look, and that reflection gave her, she now discovered, a sense of power and exaltation.

She put out her cigarette and went to the ladies' room, aware but uncaring of the other women's eyes upon her. Inside the empty tiled room a mirror ran along and over the gleaming bank of white sinks. She stood there and regarded herself under the bright fluorescent light. Her eyes fell to her breasts. She studied them. Slowly she unbuttoned the top button on her blouse, then a second. She inspected herself quizzically. At last she rebuttoned her blouse and went back to her station. Mr. Gillespie was watching her through his doorway.

Catherine turned to her desk and forced herself into her work. A conference on the Polish economy was scheduled for Bellagio in October. October on the Italian lakes, it would take an enormous slice out of the Council's Slavic budget, but the professors, macro and micro, would love it, she reflected, especially the Poles, who didn't get many such treats. She worked straight through lunch, as she sometimes did since she didn't much enjoy the company in their small dining area off the conference room, and she knew she would not enjoy it today in particular. And she smoked two more cigarettes. Mr. Gillespie said a cautious goodbye when he left for lunch at twelve-thirty and a somewhat more outgoing hello when he returned at two-thirty smelling ever so slightly of scotch through the breath mints.

Catherine planned all along to leave the office early, and at four o'clock she switched off all peripherals and hardware on her IBM PC and turned to lock the file drawer. Mr. Gillespie was watching, as she sensed he always did. She looked up at him from the file and he looked almost as quickly, but not quite, down at his desk. It was by now a reflex on both their parts, the hunter in the office without bullets, and outside the armor-plated prey. At that point Catherine would normally have turned left in her chair, out of his line of vision, risen quickly and left. But on this bright Monday afternoon when the world ended Catherine Donovan slowly swivelled herself to the right and presented her full seated profile to the doorway. She carefully crossed her legs, which she never did to public view in the office or anywhere else. When she was sure her silent audience of one was attending, she reached down, slowly lifted the hem of her skirt and drew it back two, three four inches up along her leg. She could hear the creaking of Gillespie's chair. She ran her hand up and down the nylon on her thigh, straightening perhaps, or just possibly stroking. At length she stood up, quickly, and walked into his office.

"Mr. Gillespie, I'm about to leave for the day. Is there anything else you want?"

She recalled his face as she went down in the elevator. The strange flushed look, the tension around his mouth and eyes. He had said nothing, only nodded at her departure. Why, she wondered, did Eugene Gillespie look so painfully uncomfortable? Like the priest, only far worse. And somewhere in the back of her head, or perhaps in the pit of her belly, an answer began to take form.

Eugene Gillespie looked abruptly down at his *Times* when Catherine walked into his office the next morning. They don't like it, she thought; they really don't like it at all. She was delighted at her discovery. Men could not handle the weapon that they themselves had invented and had been using on her all of her life. She stood there in front of him, one hand negligently on her hip, the other lying along her thigh. They talked about the conference, as they always did these days, but now her eyes followed his. They were on her face as they talked, but she had no more than to rub her fingers slightly, almost imperceptibly, against the shiny surface of the dress on her thigh and his eyes would fall there, and then move suddenly, guiltily, away. Catherine was in a marvelous mood all day.

Jesus, Mr. Hopper observed to himself as he sipped his martini in the library, old Tom Donovan must have really stuck it to her last night.

On Wednesday Catherine summoned up her courage and decided to try the same maneuver on far less familiar terrain, the doorway of the rattan and hemp decorated office of Mr. Coulson. Langston Coulson had once been caught in a minor and generally harmless revolutionary exercise in Honduras, which is why he may have stared somewhat longer and evenly than Eugene Gillespie. But the travails of Central America, it turned out, were no better preparation for the pointedly displayed body of Catherine Donovan than were the intricacies of the Polish economy, and whatever fantasies he might have entertained in private, they and he ended in an embarrassed and whimpering retreat. And yes, fear. She had caught its scent. Catherine was so elated that she rewarded Mr. Gillespie with an extra ration of thigh before she left for the day. And when he too finally composed himself and left, he stopped off in Grand Central and had two drinks before boarding a later train for Rye.

Catherine always walked home from work, ten blocks down Third Avenue to Twenty-ninth, then one over to Lexington. She walked that and every other stretch of New York streets with her gaze cast down, evasive of all eye contact. She heard the sounds, of course. Those she could not evade, the clicking, whistling, hissing, the terrible sucking and smacking of lips. They had shocked and enraged her when she first heard them at fourteen, and if the shock was long gone, the rage burned more brightly and fiercely than ever. If I had a gun, she often thought, I would kill them.

She did have a weapon now, she reflected as she walked along this Wednesday afternoon. It could control, intimidate. But not everyone. Why not? She had no answer. Why could she give the merest suggestion of herself to Gillespie or Coulson and they would back off in sheeplike fear, while the clickers and the suckers along the street would cry in joy and derision if she did the same to them? Would they? Was it class, conditioning, some nuance of machismo that she had missed?

It does not do to become distracted in New York City. Catherine was standing waiting for a red light on the corner of Thirty-first Street when she was jolted from her thoughts by a hand resting upon, then gently but unmistakably squeezing her hip. Her reaction was instinctive and authentic. Already half-sick with anger, she whirled and raked her bared nails across the face of the man standing beside and behind her. His hand went to his bleeding face in shock and pain. Briefly they locked eyes. He felt the full force of her rage upon him, turned and bolted back up Third Avenue.

Catherine crossed the street and stood shaking against the building on the opposite corner. A voice next to her said, "You want some dickie, Miss? Nice for you. Big. Here, feel." She turned again, this time away from the voice, and ran down Third

Avenue, across Twenty-ninth, into her apartment building. She slammed her fist against the elevator button. She was still shaking when she tried to put her key in her door lock. Inside she tore off her clothes, left them on the floor where they fell, and plunged panting and sick into the shower.

Catherine was newly dressed and sitting in the bedroom when Tom came home at last. She did not look up; she did not return his greeting.

"What's wrong?" he asked from the doorway and started across the room to where she was sitting.

"Don't come near me," she threatened.

He stopped where he was.

"Why? What happened?"

He could imagine many things that might have happened, some of his doing and some not. He looked at her. He could see nothing.

"I was assaulted on my way home from work today."

"Assaulted? My God, Catherine, did you tell the police? Did they bring you home?"

"They wouldn't do anything."

"What do you mean they wouldn't do anything? Assaulted where? By who?"

He was now standing at her side.

"The filthy, vicious, stupid pig. I loathe them all."

He looked at her thoughtfully.

"Catherine, did somebody, some man, touch you on the street?"

She turned her head away.

"I don't want to talk about it, if you don't mind."

He expelled a long and futile stream of breath.

"Come outside, Catherine, so we can talk. Not about this. About something else."

He turned and went into the living room. She followed him after a while.

"Don't worry about dinner," he said. "We'll go to the Chinese restaurant. Catherine?" He paused. "This is going to be very difficult."

She looked at him. She too could imagine many things, some of her doing and some not.

"There's something wrong," he said carefully. "We've been over it all before. Not between us, but, if you'll forgive me, something wrong in you. Some fear or terror. And I don't think it has anything to do with me, as a person."

She continued looking at him without expression.

"It can't be pleasant for you, the fear," he went on. "I've been afraid at times too, and so I know it's not easy to take. Do you want to do something about it?"

"Like what?" she asked.

It was not an entirely friendly question on her part. It may have had some small trace of curiosity in it, but there were even broader strains of suspicion and anxiety in her voice.

"Would you like to see an analyst?"

She lay down on the couch in an almost unconscious parody of his question. Her eyes roamed the ceiling.

"Did Maddy tell you to say that?"

"No," Tom said, "Maddy did not tell me to say that. It's my idea. Why? Did you ever talk about it with her?"

"Before we were married she mentioned it to me every five minutes or so. Now she seems to have stopped."

Her eyes finally came to rest on some invisible point above her.

"Have you slept with Maddy yet?"

Neither said anything for a very long time.

Finally, she sat up on the couch.

"I'll fix dinner," she said. "It's cheaper than going out. And I'll see an analyst, if that's what you want."

Seven

Catherine wasn't crazy about Neil Astrakhan by any means, and she was even less taken by the idea of going every Monday after work from East Thirty-ninth Street to West Tenth Street. It was too far to walk and so she had to shuttle from Grand Central to Times Square and then take the Sixth Avenue express to West Fourth Street. Catherine loathed the subway.

"Don't worry about it," Maddy assured Tom. "It's just the normal resistance pattern. And sooner or later she's going to discover Balducci's food palace on the corner. I'll bet you'll be eating better on Monday nights from now on."

"Make yourself comfortable," Neil Astrakhan said at her first visit. "You can sit in the armchair or lie on the couch or walk around or just stand, whatever you want, just so long as you don't harm the furniture or me or yourself."

"I'll sit, thank you."

She sat in the armchair angled to his own, both feet planted firmly on the ground.

"Well?" he began.

"Well what?" she said. "I've never been in therapy before."

"Well, you're here now and you're paying seventy-five dollars for forty-five minutes. You can spend it reading or looking out the window or we can talk."

"I'm here because my husband wanted me to come."

"Do you think he should be here with you?"

"No."

"Why not?"

"He has no problems."

"And you, do you have problems?"

"Is this what it's going to be like?" she sighed.

Neil Astrakhan threw back his head and laughed.

"God, I hope not," he said, still laughing.

He looks Armenian, Catherine thought. Dark black hair salted with gray and with a bushy moustache to match.

"Are you Armenian?"

"Oh, I forgot to tell you," he said. "You can ask me whatever you want to too. Fair is fair. But don't waste too much time on me. I'm not paying. No, I'm not Armenian. Close, though. Georgian."

"What is Georgia famous for?"

"Shashlik, wine and lots of trouble."

She relaxed a little in the chair.

"And you're Irish Catholic, I assume. What was your maiden name?"

"O'Rourke. Yes, both of us are."

"Would your father be very upset if he knew you were here, in a psychiatrist's office?"

"Probably. But he's dead. Ten years. My mother's still alive. In Queens."

"Catholic schools?"

She told him about her schools, and as her guard came

70

down, about her job and eventually even how she met Tom Donovan. It was all very smooth-planed, he noticed. No ripples, no comments and few clues as one session flowed into the next.

"Why don't you try lying down on the couch," he suggested. "Then you wouldn't have to look at me all the time."

"I like to see who I'm talking to."

"You also like to gauge reactions," he said. "You steer with your eyes."

"I prefer to sit."

"As you wish. Tell me something, Catherine. What's the worst thing you can imagine happening to you?"

There was a long pause. He had taken her by surprise. The mask of her face dissolved into a series of agitated frowns.

"Lose my job," she said at last.

"I don't believe you," he said. "Would that be worse than getting divorced, for example?"

She gave no sign.

"Than getting raped?"

She twisted abruptly in the chair. Her upper body turned one way, her tightly clenched knees contorted sharply the other, away from him. She drew her long black hair across her face like a veil.

"Catherine, nobody thinks rape is terribly pleasant."

"Don't say that word to me."

"Have you ever been raped?"

Her hand went up to her mouth. Too late. She vomited on his blue armchair and on his purple and green carpet.

After she left Neil Astrakhan called Tom at the PA and told him that Catherine was slightly ill, nothing more serious than an upset stomach, and that she might be too embarrassed to come to the next session, which was all right.

"Just go easy, Tom," he said. "She'll be OK."

She did come to the next session, however, defiance written all over her face and frame, and sat herself down on the couch.

"How are you feeling?" he asked.

"Fine. Why?"

"Don't you remember being sick last time?"

"I may have been a little upset," she said, "but I'd hardly call it being sick."

"We have different recollections, I guess."

"I guess," she said as she arranged herself comfortably on the couch.

"You were telling me how you met Tom."

She went back to the New School. And Maddy.

"Is that the Maddy I'm supposed to know?" he asked.

"Yes. Do you?"

"Well, after a fashion," he smiled. "She and I had a little flirtation, you might say, during the last blackout."

Catherine's eyes narrowed. She shifted on the couch.

"Was she your patient at the time?"

"No," he smiled again, "Maddy was never my patient. We met downstairs in the lobby." He watched as she grew more agitated in the chair. "And in case you're wondering, we did have sex in this office. Right on that couch where you're sitting."

Catherine abruptly stood up and went to the window where she stood staring into the street.

"Why does that upset you, Catherine? Because she's your friend or just the thought of the physical sex act?"

"Neither," she said and returned to the armchair.

"Do you admire Maddy?" he asked.

"How can I talk about her when you've slept with her?"

"Does that make her a non-person?"

"No, of course not. It's just that there's some violation of confidence. I'm not sure where, but somewhere." She looked at his diplomas on the wall. "Are you married?"

"No," he said. "Not now."

She said nothing, merely continued to inspect his walls.

"Do you believe in marital fidelity?" he asked.

"What do you mean by that?"

72

"No sex outside of marriage."

"Why must we always talk about sex?" she said with a frown.

"All right, Catherine, you talk about whatever you wish."

She stared straight ahead.

"Do you have any brothers or sisters?" he asked after a while.

"No."

"As a matter of fact you have an older brother. Did you forget him?"

"He left the family."

"Another non-person. What's his name?"

"You probably know his name."

"Yes, I do," he said. "I just wanted you to say it."

She said nothing.

"How many words or names can't you say, Catherine?"

"If I could say them, then I'd know how many there were, wouldn't I?"

"Time's up. Look, Catherine, I'd like you to start writing down your dreams as you remember them. Try to do it first thing in the morning, when you get up. All right?"

"I'll try," she said.

At first there was nothing. She said she didn't dream. Then tiny fragments began to surface.

I dreamed I was at work and I couldn't find my raincoat. I thought everyone was looking at me.

I dreamed I was walking along Third Avenue and suddenly I wasn't wearing shoes. Everybody laughed.

I dreamed Tom was an alcoholic.

I dreamed . . . I dreamed . . .

"Do you ever go around the house without clothes?"

"Never."

"When you lived at home?"

She bit her lip.

"No, certainly not."

"What do you wear to bed, Catherine?"

"A nightgown. What do you wear to bed, doctor?"

"Nothing, as you probably guessed. And you change in the bathroom?"

"Of course. Why not?"

"You know, Catherine, since you came in here this evening you've been playing with the buttons on your blouse. What do you think that means?"

"It means I'm nervous. I'm often nervous, as you've probably noticed."

"Do you want to take it off?"

"Is that what *you* want, doctor?"

"On one level, yes, of course. You must know you're very tempting."

Neil Astrakhan sat and inspected the palm of his hand. "Tempting" was for him an unusual but appropriate choice of word. Had Catherine Donovan at last convicted him of the knowledge of sin?

Her steady gaze was still full on his face.

"But," he continued, "I don't think it would help your therapy if you did, even if you wanted to."

"You're trying to seduce me, aren't you, doctor?"

"No, I don't think so. But you may have a better instinct for such things," he said. "What makes you think so?"

"All the talk about sex. All men do it. They float you their favorite subject to see how you'll react. They know it embarrasses girls, that they don't like to hear such things."

"That's very interesting."

"I've had to listen to that kind of talk all my life," she went on. "Since I was a little girl. Boys, even grown men, used to wait until I came into the room and then start talking about it because they knew I'd cry and run away."

"That's terrible," he said quietly. "That's a terrible thing to do to a little girl."

"I remember when I was eleven one of my brother's friends

held me and they all took turns saying the most filthy things they could think of. And when I was older, no, younger, I can't remember, they opened their pants and made me look at them."

"Did they touch you?" he inquired gently.

She shook her head violently. It was gone. Eradicated.

"You know, sometimes I'd like to be like Maddy, I think."

"How so?"

"She seems so relaxed. At ease. She does what she wants and it doesn't seem to bother her."

"That's a nice way to be," he said. "But then again, she probably envies the fact that you're married and she's not."

"It's more than that," she said. "I see her looking at Tom when we're all together and I can almost read her mind. I'd be better with him than Catherine is."

"Maybe it's your own mind you're reading. He did marry you after all. You must give him something she couldn't."

"Or he thought I could," she said sadly.

"He's still with you. Don't be so self-deprecating."

She nodded in agreement.

"Does he give you everything you want, Catherine?"

"Yes, he's very kind and patient."

"Is that all you want from him?"

"Well, it helps."

"It surely does," he said. "Would you ever like to have children?"

"Someday, maybe."

"Catherine, how often do the two of you have intercourse?"

He didn't much care for the word, but it was the only one he felt she would or could accept.

"Not very often."

"Once a month? Every six months?"

Her eyes moved over the tracery in the carpet.

"What would you do if I did take off my blouse?" she suddenly asked.

"Now who's floating sex for a reaction?" he said gently. "To

75

say nothing of changing the subject. Sex does have its uses, you see."

She smiled, then looked up and directly into his eyes.

"We never have intercourse," she said, her voice rising slightly. "He's never fucked me, not even once."

She did it, she thought. She told him, though she swore she would never tell anyone. And she used that word.

"You made me do that, to tell you," she accused him next time.

"Catherine, your life is a conspiracy. Everyone is trying to make you do something you don't want to do. Does it ever occur to you that there are things you do want to do but that you're too frightened to take on the responsibility for and so you shift it to someone else?"

"I do everything I want. I am responsible for my life."

"Catherine, are you asking me to believe that you don't want to sleep with your husband? Or is he the one who is unwilling?"

"No, it's me," she confessed. "Why do you think I'm here?"

"You never did say, Catherine."

"I don't want to do it," she went on. "If I did, I would."

"That sounds very simple."

"Oh, it is, doctor. It's a filthy, degrading act. Every man on the street wants to do it, like dogs. They think of nothing else. They're always looking, suggesting, putting out their hands, as if I were a piece of goods."

"Is that the way Tom treats you, like a piece of goods?"

She thought about that for a while.

"No," she said at last. "He loves me. He truly does."

"Then why shouldn't he *make* love to you? And you to him?"

"Sex is not love. You don't have to *make* love."

"Maybe not, but it's not hate either, do you think?"

76

"I think maybe it is. I think men do it because they hate women; they want to hurt them."

I dreamed I was in church. The priest opened his cassock and he had no clothes on underneath.

I saw a man expose himself on the West Fourth Street subway station. The people ran up and started to beat him.

A man standing on Thirty-fourth Street looked me up and down and said, "You're some juicy piece of cunt," after I passed. I turned and ran back and dug my nails into his eyes. Deep in. They felt like jelly. No blood, just jelly.

I saw Tom in bed with another woman. They were both naked. He had an immense penis, the size of my arm, and he took it in his hand like it was an artificial limb and slowly put it into her vagina. It must have hurt her horribly,but she didn't say anything. She just smiled and he smiled. I stood and watched. I think they knew I was there.

I bought a large pink dildo, it was very embarrassing, and I use it to masturbate.

"What do you think about when you masturbate, Catherine?"

"What? What are you talking about?" she said frowning.

"You just said you masturbated."

"No I didn't. I never touch myself and I certainly wouldn't do that other thing."

"Sorry," he said. "I thought you said you did. Do you think it's a sin?"

"I don't believe any of that stuff any more. All they told us were lies."

She thought of the time, a couple of months ago, when she made her first timorous entry into the dark interior of Saint Agnes's. She was curious, she told herself, how she would feel being in that once so familiar environment after so many years away. She sat in the shadows by the guttering candles and stared at the altar, at the opaque stained glass windows, smelled all the old scents of the past, like the rank sea. Star of the Sea. Stella Maris. She never understood what that meant. Something about sailors. There were boats in Bayside, but none of them belonged to her family. Her brother Gerald sailed, or at least he lay around the decks of boats and swilled beer with his friends. They had cabins downstairs, narrow places with a kitchen and bunks and a tiny porthole where you could see the sky as you lay on the bed, a woolen blanket itchy on your back. And the confessionals. Dark booths where you had to kneel and tell all. All.

"Bless me, Father."

She even remembered how it began.

Eight

She sat on the IND express as it headed south down Sixth Avenue from Forty-second Street. Shredded newspapers drifted across the deeply stained floor. Catherine watched them eddy back and forth near her feet. Tom was right, she thought. She wasn't telling Doctor Astrakhan everything. He had already forced a lot out of her, more than she wanted to say really, but she had not told him about what had happened in the Saint Agnes Rectory or the new and dangerous way she was beginning to treat men at the Council.

Catherine lifted her eyes to her fellow passengers. An elderly Chinese lady sat slumped and stolid directly opposite her. On the woman's left was a well-dressed man with a portfolio in his lap, and on the other side a young black man in green trousers and half-laced sneakers. The well-dressed man was reading the ads above her head, but the black man was staring directly at her, relaxed and lethargic. No, too dangerous by far. She shifted her body slightly toward the man in the suit and his eyes came down to hers. She immediately broke the contact, looked directly ahead at the Chinese woman, then down at her own palms, which were damp with perspiration. She never perspired, she thought. She moved her hands slightly on her lap, slowly hitching her skirt up and over her knees. She could feel her hands trembling.

At Thirty-fourth Street the Chinese woman and the suited man with portfolio got up and left through the center door. Catherine clenched her hands and quickly shifted her body back to center. What am I doing, she groaned to herself. This was dangerous, she knew, more dangerous than anything she had done in her life, but it carried with it a sense of exhilaration so powerful that she was almost incapable of resisting. She would have to resist. She would have to stop. She bit her lip till she could feel the pain.

The train slowly left the Thirty-fourth Street station. Catherine looked up again. The young black man was still staring, aimlessly, distractedly, in her general direction. Don't! Don't! she pleaded with herself. Her eyes moved farther down the car. The man in the suit who had been sitting across from her now stood leaning against the far door, his eyes upon her, a silent smile on his lips. He must have gotten back on the train, she thought in near panic. When he saw she had noticed him, he slowly began to move down the car toward her. She had a sudden impulse to bolt, but before she could move he sat himself down directly opposite her. She could see from the tops of her eyes his fingers drumming insistently on the leather portfolio on his lap.

Her hands moved once again cautiously on her lap and her skirt inched upward back toward her knees, then over. Slowly her knees parted, just a fraction. She now looked fully into his face. He was no longer smiling. He looked as tense as she, as taut and as anxious as Gillespie or Coulson. He was waiting, as

80

they had. Another fraction of separation between her legs, now in perfect and knowing consciousness. Another. It was as if there was an absolute silence, an absolute emptiness in the car. Just herself and the man tranfixed opposite. She felt herself getting dizzy, felt the flush in her face, the trembling in her thighs. Another fraction of opening. Now she could feel the air swirling between her legs, drafting up into her hidden parts.

West Fourth Street. It took them both by surprise. Catherine rose quickly and hurried out the door, aware that he was somewhere behind her as she moved headlong down the platform.

"Miss?"

She kept walking.

"Miss?"

He was now next to her, walking rapidly in step. They walked together without speaking to the exit. Up on the street he got in front of her. She stopped.

She had looked at him on the train but not seen him. Now she inspected the man before her. He was perhaps forty-five, sandy-haired, neither attractive nor ugly. A man, just a man.

"I wonder," he began uncertainly, "I wonder if you'd like to have a drink with me?"

Catherine smiled to herself. Is that it, you silly stupid man? Her anxiety began to drop off.

"I'm afraid I can't do that," she said as politely as he. "I have an appointment and I'm already late."

"How long will it be? Maybe we could have a drink afterwards."

She looked at her watch.

"About an hour."

"Do you want to have a drink then? There's a place right up the block called Mary Lou's. I could meet you there."

"That sounds fine."

He grinned broadly.

"What's your name?" she asked.

"Michael."

"I'm Carol. That will be fine, Michael. I'll see you in an hour at Mary Lou's and we'll have a nice talk together."

It sounded for all the world like a date at a Sunday school picnic.

Catherine waited until he was gone and then continued up to Tenth Street.

"What's the matter?" Neil Astrakhan asked. "You seem very preoccupied this evening. Something on your mind?"

Yes, as a matter of fact there was. Catherine Donovan was wondering if Carol, the subway tramp, would ever have the courage to take on this cool moustached man in the three-piece suit who pulled her wisdom teeth early every Monday evening.

She fingered the top button on her blouse.

No, she thought. If she tried her powerful new medicine on Neil Astrakhan, he would find some way to make her pay. He would strip her naked and make her look at herself. She shuddered at the imagining.

"No," she said. "It's just that a man tried to pick me up on the subway just now."

"I guess he didn't know who he was dealing with," Neil Astrakhan said. "Maybe you should wear a sign. A bi-lingual sign for the subway."

"I don't think that's very funny."

Later on the street she blew a small kiss, a tiny kiss really, in the direction of Mary Lou's.

Bye-bye, Michael. Enjoy your drink.

"What is this?" her husband asked still later over dinner.

"Prosciutto bread. I got it at Balducci's. Is it good?"

"It's dynamite. If there is a God, He's most certainly made of starch. Pasta, pizza, lasagna, french fries, rye bread, the evidence is unmistakable."

"You forgot croissants."

"Croissants. Of course, the clincher. How could I ever have forgotten croissants."

Catherine chewed reflectively on her veal cutlet, remote from all theological concerns.

"Tom? Have you ever picked up anybody?"

"What kind of question is that? You man like a woman?"

"I'm not asking you about your social life, believe me, just about the technique. How do you do it, does one do it? How does it work?"

"Well, not to descend to particulars, dearest, it's a question of getting their attention first. If they're already looking at you, that's one thing; if not, that's much tougher. I don't know, it all depends."

She put down her fork and rested her chin on her hands.

"If you're in a bar, you see," he continued, warming a little to his theme, "you just slide up and say, 'Hi. I'm Bruno.' And she says either, 'Hi. I'm Suzie,' or 'Get lost, creep.' Somewhere else, you've got to establish eye contact, I guess, somehow get her attention in some unthreatening way."

"And how do you do that?" she wanted to know.

"Beats me. But I know what you don't do. You don't call out or whistle or shout."

"Then what are all those men trying to do out on the streets, the ones who make the noises? Aren't they trying to pick up women?"

"God no. They'd drop dead if you ever walked over to them and said, 'OK, mister, I like your style. Let's fuck.' No, they're just trying to harass, to get a little rise out of someone who can't fight back."

"A *little* rise?" she protested. "I'd kill them if I could get my hands on them."

"Catherine, dearest, you're the kind of patsy that construction workers and delivery boys pray for. Why do you let them get so much under your skin?"

83

If he were a woman, she thought, he'd understand all right.

"How about prostitutes?" she continued. "How do you pick up a prostitute?"

"Catherine, you don't pick up a whore."

"Please don't use that word, Tom. I don't like it."

"OK, whatever you call them, you don't pick them up. They're out there waiting for *you*. That's their job."

"Have you ever had a prostitute? I mean before we were married."

He wasn't exactly sure of Carlie's professional status, but he thought he'd give it a pass anyway.

"No."

"Do you think it must be exciting," she pursued, "paying for it?"

Was she talking to Grace? No, of course not. Don't imagine trouble, he warned himself.

"You're very interested in this, aren't you, Catherine? Are you thinking of fighting them or joining them?"

A cloud suddenly descended over eyes that had been shining brightly with excitement only seconds before.

"Tom, that's not funny."

"It's your subject, not mine," he said as he rose from the table, their dinner plates in his hands. "What time is Maddy picking us up?"

"Eleven, I think."

"My God, doesn't that woman ever go to bed?"

This was Maddy's party, or at least she seemed to be issuing most of the invitations to this slam-bang up someone else's alley. The someone else was Harry, last name, occupation and occasion of celebration unknown, as was customary with Maddy. "C'mon. You're invited to a blast at Harry's" was the entire protocol. And then, as a postscript, "Pick you up at eleven."

When Catherine and Maddy first met, the former Miss O'Rourke used to express the normal human curiosity about who she might expect to meet, where, under what circumstances, how dressed. In vain. "Oh, people" or "Wear anything" were the only clues Maddy ever let drop. A Maddy summons was as mysterious as an invitation to the Transfiguration, and often quite as sensational in the sequel.

Maddy buzzed them from downstairs at eleven forty-five, well within the parameters of what Miss Kirsch understood as "eleven o'clock." They descended, Tom in sweater and jeans, Catherine in a white blouse with black skirt. Maddy was leaning smoking against a cab at the curb. She was wearing a beaded dress with a feather in her hair. Catherine gave her a dark look of feminine betrayal.

"Why not?" Maddy shrugged, and they headed downtown in the cab, Tom wedged in the middle, Maddy with her left knee pressed familiarly against his, Catherine attempting to remove her right breast from beneath his probing elbow. He lived, he sighed to himself, in a topsy-turvy but highly predictable universe.

"This is it," Maddy commanded at last.

"The New York Stock Exchange?" Tom said.

"Sure," Maddy said without apparent concern, though Tom knew there was delight coursing through every nerve of her acrobatic body. "Harry has a seat. And it's unoccupied at night."

"We're going to get arrested, I can feel it," Catherine said.

"I have a friend there too," Maddy said cheerfully as she hopped out onto the sidewalk.

They were let into the darkened building by a uniformed guard who required no other identification than Maddy's breezy, "Hi there. How's it goin'." They climbed two flights of echoing marble stairs and Maddy led them down a dark hall to what seemed, at this remove, a muffled roar.

"Notice the muffled roar," Maddy said. "That's us."

It said only "Harold Plunkett, Esq. Member" on the bronze plate affixed to the oaken door.

"Former member," Tom said.

They went in. The roar was no longer muffled. It issued

85

from two large speakers set up in the business quarters of
Harold Plunkett, Esq. The speakers were made of pine; everything else in the room wore a three-inch plate of venerable oak
and leather. Earlier, less imaginative Plunketts hung on the
walls, their disapproval of their scion happily anticipated by
death.

"Christ!" Tom exclaimed softly.

"Go," Maddy commanded and gave him a furtive thwump
on his astonished behind.

It was not immediately apparent which one of the assem-
bly, if any, was the estimable Member and no one seemed very
much to care. Rather, it was the remarkable combination of
business suits and Mohawk haircuts, of Brooks Brothers' serge
and Kaufmann camouflage that seized the mind and the eye. It
was a carefully stirred cocktail of the Two Cultures, a nostalgic
brew of Radical Chic with a creamy topping of coke and other
spices of a rarer sort. It was familiar and it went down easy.

"You come with me," Maddy said and led Tom off by the
arm.

Catherine was not at her best at parties, and she felt a rush
of panic and then a rapidly mounting anger at being left standing
alone in the middle of the thick piled carpet.

"Want a drink?" a voice inquired at her elbow within thirty
seconds of her desertion. What Catherine never realized was
that she was marked and entered on male agenda from the moment she entered any room.

She turned slowly to face her new tormentor. He was what
anyone else would have judged a pleasant-looking young man
from the business side of the Great Divide, luckier than most
perhaps, since he happened to be standing nearest when
Catherine Donovan was tossed overboard to fend for herself.

"I don't drink," she answered briefly.

"How about a Perrier?"

Catherine stood, uncertain of her course.

"It only comes in one flavor," he said with a grin.

86

"I'm not thirsty."

She turned and walked off, toward a table which looked like it might have food on it. So it seemed, but she couldn't identify any of it, except that it was likely fish and that it was quite possibly raw. Not uncooked. Just raw. She stood contemplating the entire unappetizing melange dredged up from the black depths of the Sea of Japan.

"Not very good looking, is it?"

They have to get your attention first, she remembered, in some unthreatening way.

She looked up. He had her attention.

Across the room Maddy slipped her hand into Tom's rear jeans pocket and let it rest against his no longer astonished flesh.

"How's it goin'?" she said cheerily.

"Maddy, the last time you used that same opening with me you got laid, remember?"

"So, how's it goin?" she repeated, her cheeriness not a whit diminished.

"Maddy, be careful," he pleaded.

"Don't worry. I'll take precautions, as they used to say. My bed or hers?"

"That's really not much of a joke, you know," he said.

"No, I suppose not." The cheeriness had evaporated. "God damn! Who invented monogamy?"

"Some woman, I'd guess," he said.

"No one ever explained it to me that way before, Thomas. In that case I'm for monogamy, I guess." She sipped her drink thoughtfully. "How's the therapy going?"

"How do I know?" he shrugged.

"Can't you see any change?"

"Yes, she likes to talk about whores. Though not by name."

"Well, that's a change. Is she for or against?"

"She's still making up her mind."

Catherine stood fingering the button on her blouse.

"Yes," her new companion said, his gaze fatally wandering

somewhere off over her head, "in my shop we're looking for a three to one split, with options right down the line. You guys got any money in paper? What did you say your husband did?"

The broker had paddled to her side across the sea of raw fish, but Catherine was now looking, with options right down the line, at another catch, a blond young man with rimless glasses who stood at the other end of the buffet table and was inspecting what appeared to be a seaweed aspic. He looked up, a piece of the stuff in his hand, and found Catherine Donovan's dark eyes upon him. He hastily looked away.

Him. That's the one, she thought.

"Excuse me," she said to the broker in the very middle of one of his enriching explanations and made her way toward the end of the table.

"Hello. My name is Catherine," she said from behind the blond man's shoulder.

He quickly shifted his seaweed from right hand to left, thought better of it, and put his wet right hand behind his back.

"Er, yes. Hello. I'm Alex."

She had served but she didn't know how to rally. She stood shifting from one foot to the other.

"Do you like seaweed?" he asked.

He hadn't played much mixed singles either.

"No, not really."

This is a disaster, she thought. I don't know how this works. I never will.

"Here," he said, "let me give you some of the other things. Some of them look like they might be edible."

He got a plate, made a selection—"I think this thing here is possibly poisonous" he said at one point—and handed it to Catherine.

"I'm not very hungry," she said with a wan smile.

"What in the world has that got to do with it?" he said.

She picked delicately, and in perfect ignorance, at a sea spider.

88

They stood and chewed in silence for a while.

"Alex," she tried, "did I pick you up?"

"Lord no," he said. "How could you? I'm gay."

She continued chewing and then, when there was no further recourse short of spitting it out onto her plate, she swallowed whatever it was that was in her mouth.

"May I ask you a question?" she said when she had recovered somewhat.

"Certainly," he said as he spit his own portion onto his plate. "As long as it isn't rude."

"Can't you or won't you?"

He lit a cigarette to kill the taste in his mouth.

"Can't I or won't I *what*?"

"Have sex with a woman."

He blew the smoke from his cigarette past her ear.

"Put it this way," he said. "I prefer not to."

She briefly thought he must be the happiest man alive, someone free to indulge his preferences. Or the biggest liar.

"And you?" he asked.

"I can't."

He had expected a wisecrack, some clever evasion from this girl with the long dark hair and the deepset eyes. But he knew what he had gotten instead was some sad and painful truth.

He looked around the room, in part because he had finished with her and in part to relieve his sudden embarrassment at this intimacy with a stranger. Catherine read the glance otherwise.

"My husband is the one over there with the woman's hand in his pants pocket."

Nine

"Promise me, Catherine, that you'll at least try to be nice to this guy. Just smile or something."

"I thought we were just going to look at some clothes?"

"I know," Maddy sighed. "But our Mr. Stern likes you to smile when you're looking at his dresses. Not at the dresses, at him. Got it?"

Catherine Donovan, she knew, would never get it.

Ari Stern, soldier turned entrepreneur, confronted Bloomingdales's as directly as he once had the grenadiers of the Syrian Third Army: he set down his sassy and underpriced boutique right across Lexington Avenue from the Great Power. And once again the tactic worked. Streams of deserters forded the avenue at Fifty-ninth or Sixtieth and emerged, moist and eager and smiling on the doorstep of Pretty Things. "Come in,"

Ari smiled back at the ladies and flashed a drastically reduced designer dress or skirt or blouse, its label cut slyly in half, to ease their entry.

Maddy Kirsch was practically a sabra in that promised land. Three months after Ari Stern had invoked the Law of Bail Out from Eretz Israel and emigrated to Dry Dock Country, she was deep in his racks, running her hands over sleeve lines and under hems, twisting price tags, fingering those half-labels with ill concealed desire.

Owner and customer had noticed each other immediately, of course, in the manner of two old pros. She thought a new hairstyle might undo some of the damage of ten years trying to look like Tony Curtis; he thought she would be terrific in bed. Nice back on the man, tough arms, cute ass, she observed across the ranks of tailored suits. His reflections from behind the counter were at once more global, more philosophical. I'll take it. Probably has a loud mouth, Maddy concluded. Right now, Ari Stern promised himself.

"The prices marked on the tags are not engraved on stone like the Ten Commandments," he said from her side.

I assumed not, she thought to herself, but your intentions are.

"Want to cut a little deal?" she suggested.

"Sure, just for you," he said in his best Tony Curtis manner.

Early Tony Curtis, she thought.

"You take a tad off the price of this suit and I'll buy it. How's that deal grab you?"

"One more condition."

"Sure, Tony, anything you say."

"That you come back another time. And my name is Ari."

"You've made yourself a deal, Ari. You got good goods here."

"I like only the best."

"How very wise of you. And I think I'll just try this little number on while you're still perspiring."

Maddy held up her end. She went back, and often, and she kept whittling, smoothing down prices on the sandpaper edge of Ari Stern's expectations. He was wise enough not to overcommit to this one campaign, of course, and as Maddy fingered her way along the Anne Kleins, she noted that other deals were being struck behind the Laurens and the Chanels, often with tawny, long-legged ladies of a type rarely found on the kibbutz in Galilee where Ari Stern had sweated away his idealism until at thirty-five there was no more left. The dream of Zion had yielded to other dreams, some of them of tawny, long-legged ladies fresh off the boat from Bloomingdale's.

Ari suffered rejection with all the practiced indifference of the shrewd lifetime gambler. If not this one, then maybe the next, he figured. Or the one after that. But like all true gamblers, he was sometimes careless of the odds. No tawny lady ever tumbled for the tumbling prices; all Ari Stern got for his pains were girls in jeans and Jordache blouses whom he could have had for list.

And Maddy sized it up with an eye as shrewd as Ari's own and considerably more calculating. On her second visit to Pretty Things she had decided that her own social and sexual plans had no place for a grinning, road company Tony Curtis with a graying pompador. And by the third time around she discerned that it would serve no practical end to share her decision with Mr. Curtis himself and that he had few resources to discover it on his own. So she kept Ari Stern on medium simmer and watched the prices evaporate in the heat. Maddy Kirsch was Pretty Things' chief loss-leader, and Ari Stern seemed willing to carry her on the books forever.

She was not entirely ungrateful. She rounded up her friends, Catherine among them, and led them into Ari Stern's stylish bazaar. Good deal all around, she thought. He thought exactly the same thing, particularly when he beheld Catherine Donovan, who at nothing more than first sight, and without the slightest suggestion of a smile, had five percent nicked off list for a creamy gabardine suit.

He stood before his pipe racks and watched Catherine posing before the showroom mirror.

"Very nice on you, miss. You a friend of Maddy's?"

"Yes," Catherine answered shortly. Her eyes were momentarily on the suit, but when she turned from the mirror, she caught the full force of Ari Stern's appraisal of her. There was a foolish smile on his lips, but his eyes were all business: down her shiny black hair onto her breasts, across her narrow waist, the full span of her hips, and then down carefully, lingering, to her bloomingly full and lissome legs.

Ari was programmed for such work, perhaps by too many long days in a fish cannery near Tiberias and too many long nights bivouaced in the company of men on the Golan Heights. But so too was Catherine Donovan, and her reaction was as instinctive and predictable as his own crude, wide-eyed appraisal. Her lips drew into a tight thin line, her brow creased and furrowed across her nose. There was fire in her dark eyes. She said nothing. There was no need. Ari Stern got the message as clearly and as urgently as if it had been branded on the palm of his hand: Never, you bastard. Never.

So Catherine went back to list price at Pretty Things while the more flexible Maddy's billings sank closer and closer toward the Golden Fleece whose very name none dared utter. Cost. The two of them returned together from time to time since even at list price Ari Stern could easily embarrass Big Mama's numbers across the street. But this Saturday morning on the weekend after Harold the Member's party it was not with the same easiness. Catherine had led a life of deliberately calculated ignorance of many of the unpleasant things going on around and within her, but not even her adamantine defenses could block out the knowledge that Maddy Kirsch was now stalking her husband with quite open intent.

Catherine had never seen Maddy as competition; the two played in different leagues with very different rules. Maddy was easy and even familiar with men. She publicly enticed them with her golden curls and her laughing blue eyes and then controlled them with her quick wit and ready tongue. What happened in private Catherine did not know, and Maddy, for all her love of illustrative anecdote, never gave a look into her own boudoir. It was a privilege Catherine did not crave. The bedroom was for her a terror-filled battleground, even in prospect. It smelled of lechery and lust and all the despicable desires that men harbored against her.

Catherine had a deep and relentless suspicion of men, a suspicion that masked, however imperfectly, a more deeply seated fear. She gave them no encouragement, assuredly, and so she was baffled and angry when they pursued her against her will and in despite of what were, in her mind, the clearest possible signals that what interested them—"the usual" she called it in her interior dialogs—did not in any way interest her. Catherine had no desire to compete for men; Maddy could have them all.

But as she eventually confessed to Neil Astrakhan, there was envy in the subtext of Catherine's easy surrender of the field to Maddy Kirsch. Maddy puzzled her. She seemed immune to Catherine's own suspicions and panic. Was it that she was hoodwinked by men, by their smooth seductive talk, their professed interest in none but the most spiritual congress? More likely, Catherine thought, Maddy simply saw through their pretense, led on the pretenders and in the end dismissed them with the easy contempt Catherine so wished she too could wield.

Maddy knew little of what to make of all this. Catherine had few friends, even among women, as if she suspected that men would enlist her own sex against her. In her careless way Maddy swept aside all the pretended remoteness and disinterest that Catherine first displayed toward her by dismissing it simply as nonsense. And when Catherine discovered that she could not deflect Maddy Kirsch's infectious cheer, she melted a bit and accepted the relationship. It was then that Maddy began to catch the deeper tones. In the beginning she might have thought that Catherine was indifferent to men, an eccentric view, but what the hell; she ended, however, with the conviction that Catherine O'Rourke was more interested in men than anyone she knew, and that included Maddy Kirsch.

Then Tom Donovan arrived and wooed and won Catherine O'Rourke with what seemed to the curious Maddy like remarkable ease, and, she added in a memo to her own files, without so much as a speculative glance at Maddy Kirsch. Terrific, Maddy thought, when Catherine told her they were going to marry, just what Catherine needs, a solid, attractive, reassuring man to calm her fears and loosen her limbs. She could not remember how long she thought that, six months perhaps, before she noticed the all too familiar motifs reappearing in their conversations.

"Cute guy, huh?" Maddy would suggest of someone seated on the other side of a restaurant.

"Just like all the others," was Catherine's bitter and invariable response, as if the man in question had proposed fornication on the dessert cart.

"I had an interesting date last night," she tried again. Maddy frequently had interesting dates.

"Men are disgusting," Catherine countered with a quantum leap to the conclusion of her own unstated syllogism, a syllogism whose middle term Maddy had no interest in hearing.

There is rested uncomfortably until Maddy took her cool resolve that she too deserved a piece of Thomas Donovan and that it could probably be filched without appreciable harm to the present tenant. And though Maddy's decision by now trilled openly through the public domain, so that even Catherine was aware of it, Catherine Donovan's own explosive discoveries still ran only through deep and blind underground channels.

Ari Stern greeted them at the door of Pretty Things.

"Maddy, *shalom*. Hello, Mrs. Donovan," hand to his modish hair.

"*Shalom* yourself, you grasping knave," Maddy smiled cheerfully. Ari's knowledge of English was functional but by no means perfect.

Catherine merely nodded as they passed, but if she thought that Ari Stern would omit his appraising stare, she was disappointed.

The two women parted inside the store to pursue their separate tastes, with only an occasional murmur back and forth across the racks. But Catherine watched as Ari openly stalked Maddy, as he usually did. He tracked the blond beacon of her hair up and down the aisles, one eye always carefully on the door and the hired help, while he chatted familiarly with his favorite customer.

"Maddy, when are we going to have that drink?" he cajoled.

"What's the real price of this St. Laurent dress?" she answered.

"How about Monday?"

"It says three fifty, but that must be a mistake."

"Better, I'll take an afternoon off and we'll make a day of it."

"How about two seventy-five? And I think it's spotted. Are you carrying seconds now, Ari?"

On they went as Catherine wandered among the racks with a silent and growing anger. At length she found what she wanted. White silk suit and black silk blouse in hand, she raised her voice in Maddy's direction and announced, "I'll be in the dressing room."

The ladies of Pretty Things tried on their new garments not

96

in a dressing room but in functional curtained alcoves across the back of the store. Catherine entered one at the far end and pulled the curtain behind her. Ari Stern apart, all the help and all the customers at Pretty Things were women and so most of them gave the enclosing curtain only a very perfunctory tug before changing. Not Catherine Donovan, of course. Whenever she removed part of her clothing in that or any other store, she was not content to close doors or curtains; she bolted, barred and sealed them as best she could. But not this Saturday. Six inches let the world look in on Catherine Donovan and Catherine out at the world. The world, taken in sum, could not have cared less.

The world, of course, should never be taken in sum, as Catherine knew very well. She unhooked her skirt and stepped out of it, still in the half-slip she always wore. She began to unbutton her blouse, looked up and saw, as she expected, the form of Ari Stern reflected in the full-length mirror inside the alcove. He was directly outside, two or three feet from the curtain with a full view, reflected front and fleshly back, of Catherine Donovan. She held his gaze and continued to unbutton and then remove her blouse. He moved closer to the curtain, already assured that she knew he was there and had chosen to make no sign. She stepped out of her half-slip and stood there in her shoes, bra and panties, her back to her audience of one but her expressionless face full upon his in the mirror.

He came inside the curtain and closed it behind him. The familiar trembling began in her legs and she could feel the flush once again in her face. If he touched her, she knew she would kill him. How she did not know, but she was certain she would.

He stood and looked at her, close enough for her to feel the heat of his breath. She watched his eyes sweep greedily across her shoulders, down her back, into the swell of her hips and the curve of her buttocks.

"Catherine," he said close to her ear in a voice nearly cracking with hoarseness.

"Yes?" she answered, her eyes still firm on his in the mirror, though she was quaking within.

"Let me have you."

She looked at his reflection in silence.

"I'll *give* you the suit and the blouse. Pick anything you want in the store," he pleaded.

She took the silk blouse off its hanger and put it on. Then her half slip and over it the white silk skirt and jacket.

"Take off the tags," she commanded.

He took a small scissors from his pocket and carefully snipped off the tags from both suit and blouse. Catherine folded her own skirt and blouse and put them in her handbag. She turned and walked past him into the store without a glance.

"Maddy," she called as she passed through the racks, "I'm finished here. I'll meet you in Bloomingdale's. Lingerie. Don't take too long."

Ari Stern stood, the curtain in one hand, the tags in the other, and watched her leave.

Maddy finally caught up with her in Bloomingdale's.

"What did you say to Ari back there?" she asked.

"Nothing. Why?"

"You didn't pay for the clothes."

"He said I could have them," Catherine said without looking up from the bra she held in her hands.

"He said *what?*"

"He said I could have them."

"Catherine, you're crazy."

"No, he's the one who's crazy," she said, "giving away such expensive clothes."

They walked over to Fifth Avenue in silence and then took the bus down to the Flatiron Building on Twenty-third Street.

"Catherine, what are you doing?" Maddy finally said as they stood on the sidewalk outside the freight entrance.

"What do you mean, what am I doing?"

"You're going to get yourself in trouble."

"I don't think so. And what are you doing, Maddy?" she asked. "Do you want my husband?"

"No, not any more," Maddy replied. "Do you?"

They stood looking at each other until at last Maddy shrugged and walked into the building. Catherine watched her disappear and then continued her own way down Fifth Avenue.

Catherine now smoked regularly at work, but never at home. Her cigarettes and ashtray remained in her desk at the Council and she kept careful track of her smoking. The Monday after her shopping expedition she smoked eight cigarettes, her highest daily total so far. And she passed another milestone as well. She wore her new white suit and black silk blouse to work, and this Monday there was one more undone button down the front of her blouse. Within the last two months Catherine had descended two buttons from her neck, and with the undoing of number three she, and her increasingly interested admirers, had reached somewhere toward the middle of the deep cleft between her breasts.

Mr. Gillespie noticed the new prospect on the instant, and so of course did the vigilant Mr. Hopper. Even the Messers. Coulson and Unser were aware that something had changed, though it may have taken them a trifle longer to find it. And no one volunteered to help them. Catherine Donovan had as a matter of fact disappeared from most of the private male conversations at the International Research Council. When she was publicly and unequivocally unavailable, Catherine was the frequent topic of talk in the conference room and the library, but now, when each suspected, or perhaps hoped, that she might be about to bestow herself on him in some secret and undefinable way, she disappeared from all their male chit-chat as completely as if she had evaporated.

The Council's working day drew to a close, and Mr. Gillespie sat in his office wondering if this would be a one or two drink safari to the safety of Rye and home. It all depended on the undependable Catherine Donovan and whatever she had planned for her now rutualized departure liturgy. He could hear the preparatory rustle of vestments in the sacristy outside his office, and he was assuredly in his pew behind the desk, as he now made it a point to be every day between four-thirty and five.

At four thirty-eight Catherine made a sudden appearance in his doorway.

"Mr. Gillespie," she began, "would you mind if I wore pants to the office?"

Well, for Christ's sake. His first impulse was to leap from his desk, throw himself at her feet and cry, "No, please, never cover those legs. Do you want a raise? A promotion? Name it and it's yours so long as you continue to sit there and raise your dress and feel up your thigh." On cooler reflection, however, he thought it might be better for his career and marriage to take the high ground.

"Well, I'm not sure it's entirely appropriate, pants in an office of this type."

It wasn't such terribly high ground after all; the rest of the assistants wore exactly what they pleased, from buckskin fringed chaps to spandex peddle-pushers.

"But if you wish," he generously conceded. "Of course."

And how about something tight and revealing across that gorgeous ass of yours, he added in a secret protocol to himself.

"No, it's all right. I can live without pants," she smiled as she took her leave. "Who can tell, anyway?"

It was a no-drink voyage home to Rye this day for a sober but shaken Eugene Gillespie. A beeline directly to the safe bosom of Eloise and the moppets named Jonathan and Hillary. Eloise was so startled by his premature descent into their midst that she got caught in the middle of her own secret pre-arrival vodka martini.

Catherine was herself a little disarranged from her first attempt at a speaking role on that stage where only the males had lines. Today was Astrakhan day, as Tom liked to call it, but she

100

was in no mood for questions and answers this Monday evening. Next time she would tell him she had been ill. Her period. The good Doctor Astrakhan never believed that particular excuse, Catherine reflected angrily. He belonged to the psychosomatic school on most female ailments, but it always got him talking and that was better than her spilling her guts. Yes, her period, and the hell with Neil Astrakhan this Monday.

Catherine's own homeward voyages, unfortified in the Gillespie manner by either scotch or vodka, were considerably more circumspect since her unhappy encounter on Thirty-first Street. Before leaving the Council she was always careful to go into the ladies' room and rebutton her blouse up to her neck, check her skirt, and then, once on Third Avenue, she moved quickly and observantly down the middle of the crowded sidewalk. It was no easy trick, keeping her eyes down and away from all contact and at the same time being aware of who was behind and beside her, but Catherine Donovan had both motive and considerable practice, and so she now glided southward on her low trajectory like an armed, radar-guided missile. Determined. Explosive.

She probably would have seen Ari Stern in her lobby in any event since she was always careful going into buildings. She professed not to notice him standing there chatting familiarly with her doorman, but she knew he was following her back to the elevators. She pressed the call button impatiently, he somewhat behind her and off to the side. A third person joined them in waiting. They went into the elevator, all three. The stranger left them at eight and the two, Catherine and Ari, rose to the fifteenth floor alone and in silence.

"What do you want?" she said at last.

"To talk to you, just for a while."

"I'm married. My husband is home."

They got off at fifteen.

"You're married all right, but your husband isn't at home," he said as he walked down the corridor behind her. "Your nice doorman told me he doesn't get home until seven or even seven-thirty. Lots of time, Catherine."

They were at her door.

"I don't want to talk to you. Leave me alone, do you understand?"

He looked at her, puzzled at first, then with a slowly broadening grin.

"What's the matter? You got cold feet? Lots of fun in the store but not so good at home?"

She had turned the key in the lock. With one hand he pushed the door open and with the other he propelled Catherine into the apartment.

"Now I think we have our little talk," he said as the two of them stood looking at each other in the middle of the living room.

Earlier, on the elevator, in the corridor, she thought she might be afraid, but she was not. She knew she had the resources of anger to deal with Ari Stern. He took two steps toward her.

"Don't move," she said evenly.

He stopped in his tracks, still smiling his tense and now somewhat distorted smile.

"Catherine," he said in what sounded like a conciliatory tone, "I'll give you what you want. Nice, like friends."

She said nothing. He took another step. Catherine picked up the copper ashtray on the table next to her and hurled it at his head. He dodged it easily and was quickly upon her. He stood and held her left wrist behind her, his body on hers, and struggled to get control of her right hand, which was flailing around his head. He bent and tried to kiss her, but she quickly averted her head, first to this side and then to that.

His breath was coming in rushes now, in part from the exertion and in part from his rising and self-feeding desire. He held their bodies close together and he could feel her against him and she his enlarging body upon her.

Suddenly she struck. Her right hand came across his cheek and her nails caught his left eye. He released her hand and put both his own hands to his bleeding face. For a moment Ari Stern stood there shaking and moaning while Catherine slowly backed away from him across the living room.

"Go!" she hissed at him. "Get out of this house!"

He looked unsteadily at her through the rain of his own blood. He tried to reconcile his pain, his anger and his desire. In the end it was, somewhat unexpectedly to both of them, his prudence that won out. He backed away, one hand still on his eye, and then turned quickly and left.

She stood motionless for a minute as her breath slowed and the strength came back to her knees and stomach. She looked down at her hand. There was blood on it. And his blood on the carpet. She went into the kitchen, soaked a dishtowel in cold water and tried to blot up the blood from the floor. When she thought she had gotten most of it, she went into the bedroom and removed her new black blouse, which was torn around the buttons. She took off her skirt and slip and lay down, still panting on her bed. She put her hand down to the crotch of her panties. She was all wet.

Ten

"Tom?"

A troubled Thomas Donovan looked up from his magazine. He had seen the fresh stains on the carpet, caught a drop of dark red blood on the white kitchen sink. Too troubled. Too frightened to ask.

"Um?"

"Do you think I'm attractive?" Catherine asked.

"Of course. Do you want to have sex?"

And that took care of that, as it always did. She went back to her knitting and he to his magazine, and the shifting sands soon drifted over the bloodstain on the carpet between them that Monday night.

"I'm going to bed," he announced later in the evening. "Long day tomorrow."

"OK," she said without looking up.

He went into the bathroom, removed his clothes, put on his

pajamas and brushed his teeth. She heard him climb into his bed, saw the bedroom light go off. She continued her knitting for another half hour, then Catherine too rose, took a Bloomingdale's bag from the closet and made her way into the bathroom in the dark.

She closed the door behind her and turned on the light. There were dark circles under her eyes, she noticed, as she looked unblinking at her face in the medicine chest mirror. Out of the Bloomingdale's bag she took a new lipstick, which she uncapped, smelled and then carefully applied to her pale lips. She inspected the results. She was unsatisfied with the two thin crimson lines she had drawn, redid them more thickly, arched them up and around her mouth in a broad and glossy swathe. She looked again and was content.

She removed all her clothes and then took out the new underwear she had bought on Saturday. She put on the black lace bikini panties and the black bra which mysteriously pushed her breasts up and out from underneath but had not energy left even to cover her nipples. She took down the two bathrobes from their hooks behind the door and inspected herself in the full-length mirror there. She stood, hands on her hips, legs tightly together. She could feel the warmth mounting slowly between them at the sight of her own displayed body.

She stood motionless for two, perhaps three minutes, riveted by the body in the mirror before her. She was seeing, she thought, what Ari Stern had seen, what Eugene Gillespie and Langton Coulson and certainly George Hopper would pay dearly to see, what Thomas Donovan was never permitted to see or touch. Finally, she took off the lingerie, her eyes now carefully averted from her own image, placed it back in the bag and put on her long nightgown. She carefully washed the gloss from her lips, pinned up her long dark hair and went to bed.

The following Monday Catherine Donovan once again put on her new lingerie, though not the lipstick, and in the evening went down to the office on West Tenth Street. She carefully sat

herself in the armchair and dealt them both a hand, five cards for
Neil Astrakhan and five for herself. She inspected her own with
care, uncertain of her lead.

"Do you have any cigarettes?" she asked.

He looked at her quizzically. "I didn't know you smoked."

"Sometimes," she said.

He got up, looked in his desk and brought her back an
opened pack of cigarettes.

"These your brand?"

"They'll do," she said.

He offered her one, took out his lighter and lit it for her.

"Thanks," she said and crossed her legs.

His play.

He watched her toe as it described twitching narrow arcs.

"You look like you're kicking," he said. "Is that a kick in the
balls for me?"

"Is that what it feels like?"

"Maybe," he smiled. "And I notice you didn't flinch when I
said 'balls.' "

This time she did flinch. And her toe abruptly stopped
twitching.

"Do you see Maddy often?" he continued.

"Did she call you?" she asked, frowning.

"Yes, she did."

He waited for her to continue.

"Did she tell you she's sleeping with my husband? No, she
wouldn't do that. She wanted to warn you about me, didn't she?
What was it, that I was going to get you or that I was going to get
myself into trouble?"

"What is it you're doing that's so upsetting her, do you
think?"

"Maybe it's that I've learned her little secret."

"And what is that, Catherine?"

She bit her lips, then her knuckle.

"It's easy," she said at last.

"What's easy?"

"You're easy," she said, her eyes still averted. "You're all easy."

"Who ever said we were hard? We're as easy as women, I imagine. As easy as you are."

"If you ever touch me, I'll kill you," she whispered.

His hand lay on the arm of the chair in which he sat close by her. Catherine watched it, almost as if it were disembodied, wondering if it would move.

"You often threaten to kill people, Catherine," he said, his arm still immobile on the chair. "Do you think you could?"

She said nothing.

"Do you want to kill us all? What did we do to you?"

"Nothing," she said fiercely. "How many times do I have to tell you? Nothing."

"Catherine, do me a favor. Lie down on the couch."

She smiled briefly at Neil Astrakhan and then she rose, removed her suit jacket and lay on the couch, her head near his chair.

"Like the view?" she asked. Her nipples were now clearly visible under her blouse.

"Close your eyes. Now relax and let your mind flow. Say whatever comes into your head."

A man came up to me on the street. He said, "I'm going to kill you," and took a sharp penis from his pocket and stabbed me. I was bleeding from my stomach but nobody helped me.

A man said "pussy" to me through a window and I shot him. His face disappeared.

We were sitting in a bar. You were wearing your three-piece suit and I was wearing my new underwear, which you kept staring at. We had three drinks each. I put my hand on your lap and I felt it getting hard. You said, "What do you expect, you cockteasing piece of ass?" I said nothing but I started getting hard too. You said, "You're a cunt, a hot bitch." The stuff started running down my leg and everyone saw it.

"What's the matter, can't you do it?" he asked.

She abruptly sat up.

"Do you have a piece of paper?" she said. "I'm going to write something on it, but only if you promise not to read it until after I've left."

"All right. I promise."

She took his prescription pad and wrote. She turned the pad over on its face, got up, put on her jacket and straightened her skirt and left.

"I'm all wet between my legs," he read after she was gone.

She was still wet; she could feel it as she walked up Sixth Avenue on her way home. She gazed unseeing in the shop windows as she passed. Then suddenly she stopped and retraced her steps. "Pleasures" it said on the shop window, and pleasures, or at least the means to achieve some of them, were generously displayed in the window. Catherine stood at one corner of the window and stole a cautious look at the mysterious objects there. She squinted over them and into the shop beyond. A young man sat reading behind the counter. There were no customers. She went in.

The young man looked up from his book.

"Can I help you?" he inquired pleasantly.

"Do you mind if I just look around first?"

"Sure, go ahead," he said and returned to his reading.

She moved away and inspected the objects on the walls and in the display cases, one eye always on the door in case someone should come in.

"Is someone helping you?"

A tanned middle-aged man with gray hair and dressed in jeans, a denim shirt and topsiders stood at her elbow. He had come unnoticed out of the back room.

"I'm just looking," she said nervously. She knew her voice sounded strange. It sounded strange in her own ears.

"For anything in particular?"

108

"No, I don't think so."

He continued to look at her, not with Ari Stern's crude appraisal, she thought, but with a kind of benign sexless curiosity.

She turned back to the display case.

"Maybe if you let me help you?"

She turned back to him. Someone else, a man, had come into the store.

"Forgive me," he said. "It's a long time between customers sometimes, even in the Village."

She wanted to say she wasn't a customer. That's not what she said at all, however.

"Can we go somewhere private?"

Without changing his expression he motioned her to the back. She went ahead of him through the curtain and into a small room with a desk, two chairs and stacked, unopened cartons.

"Will you sit down?" he offered.

She sat in a wooden swivel armchair.

"I'm sorry," she said. "I feel so awful." And she began to cry.

He turned, found a box of tissues on the desk and handed it to her. He let her cry until she stopped.

"I'm sorry," she said again.

"It's OK," he said. "What's wrong?"

"It's nothing. I'm all right now."

"What do you want here?" he asked, puzzled.

"I don't know."

"Look," he said gently, "you're not in the mood for this right now. Why don't I give you one of our catalogs. Then you can take it home with you and look at it when you're feeling better. And if you see something you want, you can always come back. OK?"

"OK."

He gave her a catalog from the desk and they both stood.

"My name's Bill," he said, extending his hand.

"Carol," she smiled and went out through the shop back onto Sixth Avenue.

Maddy Kirsch, that heavenly traveller, had been to Karachi and Oslo, though never to the Port Authority Bus Terminal, and by now she had heard so much about that latter place between her labelled sheets that she insisted on meeting Tom there after work that evening.

"So what's the big deal about the Port Authority?" she asked as she made herself at home in his office. "Just your standard wages of sin."

"Not exactly," he said. "Do you know we had sixty-three births in our restrooms last year."

"Really?"

"Fifty-nine in the ladies' and four in the gents'. And seventeen deaths in those same facilities. One by drowning."

"Drowning? How can you drown in a sink?"

"Who said anything about a sink?"

"God," she shuddered. "You mean somebody was murdered by being drowned in a toilet bowl?"

"It wasn't murder," Tom said. "It was ruled an accidental death. It seems the lady was attempting to wash her hair."

Maddy's reflections on that graphic scene remained unvoiced, however. Grace had strolled unannounced into the office behind her and now stood at Tom's shoulder, a sheaf of tattered worksheets in her hand.

"You want these reports?" she asked and raked Maddy with a look of both assay and dismissal much favored by the feisty *muchachas* on Ninety-sixth Street.

"What reports?"

"These, turkey," she hissed as if she had delivered a fatal Latin curse. She dropped the entire mess on his desk and took her nonchalant leave, its moral message underlined by a final small toss of her behind.

110

"The love of a Latin is indeed *volcánico,* Tom dear," Maddy observed in her usual cheery way.

"Want to eat?" he said with a sigh.

"Right *here?*" she exclaimed. "Well, if you can hack it, I guess I can. But what will La Pasionara out there think?"

"Come on," he said and escorted her smiling through the office. As she passed Grace's desk, Maddy tried one of her own hip flicks. Somehow it must not have come off; she could hear Grace cackling behind her all the way down the hall.

When they had seated themselves in a nearly deserted Thai restaurant nearby, Maddy reached across the table and took Tom's hand.

"Tom, I talked to Neil Astrakhan last week."

"I thought he didn't know you."

"Oh, he knows me all right. I was right. He *was* the guy I laid in the last blackout."

"Has he changed, or can't you tell?"

"Tom, be serious. I talked to him on the phone. It was about Catherine."

"You shouldn't have done that," Tom said mildly.

"Maybe not, but she's got me scared," Maddy said.

"Why, for God's sake?"

"I think she's wigging out. I don't know, but I can smell something coming off her."

"Like what?" he wanted to know.

"Like cunt. Rich, ripe cunt. And two weeks ago she started coming on with an Israeli guy in a store we go to."

"Catherine? With a man? Was he good-looking?"

"It doesn't matter. What does matter is that he's a gross and obvious womanizer, the kind of crude slimebucket that Catherine would normally have nightmares about."

He thought about it, tried to imagine it. All he could imagine was the bloodstain in the middle of his living room.

"Did you tell this to Astrakhan?"

"Yes," she said.

"And what did he say?"

"Nothing, naturally. But at least he knows."

"Do you think he believed you?"

"I can't tell. You never can with shrinks."

"By the way," Tom said as their food arrived, "what exactly does cunt smell like?"

"Like me," she said as she speared one of the shrimp on her plate and demurely placed it in his mouth.

Catherine never resented Tom's absences in the evening, never inquired or complained; she preferred to be alone. And when he called this evening and said he would be quite late, she was even a little relieved. She ate dinner alone and then afterward, after she had washed the dishes, she lay down on her bed with the catalog from Pleasures. But before she opened it she got up again, poured herself a large glass of chablis and only then settled down to her study.

As she turned the pages Catherine could form little idea of what she was looking at. It was more difficult than mathematics, she thought. The text beneath the drawings and photos did their best to explain, but in a language and style as alien to her as ancient hieroglyphics.

"Dildoes" the bold heading announced like a fanfare. She knew what a dildo was, or thought she did, something you put in yourself, up yourself. She stared in astonishment at the artist's renderings of what was currently available for the discriminating customer and could not imagine how anyone could conceivably. . .

On the next page was a full color photo of a model fashioned, with something more than realism, after a male organ, a very large one, it appeared, all veins and ridges, escarpments and gables. It was like the one she had been stabbed with, she shuddered, and hastily turned the page.

"A starter set?" the text coyly invited. She looked at it carefully under the bed lamp. She didn't know what the other pieces

112

were or why exactly batteries were included—oh, yes, I see—but the dildo was, if not probable, then at least possible. She tried to imagine it inside her. She could not.

She finished the wine and went into the kitchen and refilled her glass.

She lay down again on the bed on her stomach and studied pictures and text. And as her understanding grew, she slowly and unconsciously began to move her legs together, to rub her swollen pelvis against the bedspread. After a while she flipped over onto her back, turned out the light and raised her dress above her hips.

"Tom," Maddy said in her bed in the Flatiron Building, "what are you going to do?"

"Nothing," he replied. "Just let it be."

She looked down at his flushed face beneath her own.

"Are you going to get rid of her?" she asked.

"No."

"Why not, for God's sake? Oh, yes, I remember," she said as she rolled off him and onto the bed at his side. "You're trying to help her. That was it, wasn't it?"

He lit a cigarette and lay smoking in silence.

"Well, Tom, I don't buy it for a minute. In fact, I think the whole thing is pretty fuckin' sick. She's a sexual anorexic and you're her diet doctor. 'Not hungry, Catherine? OK, just don't eat. God knows I'm not going to make you.' "

Silence.

"Say something," she prodded him.

"Look, Maddy, she may have problems but she's my wife and so she's my responsibility."

"So you come here and get laid and then go home and hold her hand. Good for her. Good for you. Shit for me. What do I look like, a fucking machine?"

He looked at her. This tone, these sentiments were new to him and he did not care for either.

"Stop it," he said.

"No, I don't think I will," she said deliberately. "You love to think of yourself as altruistic, don't you? The responsible husband standing firm at the side of his bonkers wife. Well, Tom, there just happen to be other possibilities. She turns you on, doesn't she. She always has. And you know why? Because you can't have her. She's all cunt, your Catherine—the smell, you remember—and she's unavailable and it gets you off like mad. Like sleeping next to your mother nude, huh? Is that what it's like? A slut in the Flatiron Building and a nun in your own bed. Christ, it must be dynamite!"

He closed his eyes.

"But she's tripping out, your little cunt of a nun. She's getting hungry for the real thing and it ain't gonna be with you, big boy, nohow."

Sister Catherine was now standing naked, her legs spread, before her bathroom mirror. And she took the middle finger of her right hand and put it exactly where Maddy Kirsch said she never would or could.

Eleven

"Is Bill here?" she asked the young man still reading his book at the front counter of Pleasures.

"He's in the back. Shall I get him?"

He recognized Catherine from two weeks before. The nipples.

"No," Catherine said. "Why don't I just go back. What are you reading?"

"Kipling."

Bill was sitting at the desk in the back room, an open box in front of him and a piece of pink plastic in his hand.

"Hi," she said.

He looked up and smiled. "Hello, Carol. You're looking much cheerier." His eyes drifted downward toward her breasts.

By now Catherine knew exactly what her nipples looked like under a blouse. The first time she had worn the undercut lace bra was to Astrakhan's office that Monday two weeks ago.

She had kept her jacket on over her blouse all day at the Council and had removed it only inside the doctor's office. Since then she had carefully and privately studied its effect under all her blouses. Her nipples were most prominent under silk, she concluded, particularly under white and peach, when the dark aureoles glowed through the fabric around the hard pointed tips of her breasts.

Though she never did so on the street, she eventually removed her jacket at the Council. She immediately caught Astrid staring at her breasts and Sarah Wasserman too, but none of the men, she was amused to discover. They watched from afar, she was sure, but face to face they kept their eyes punctiliously above her neck. She had even stood in front of Mr. Gillespie in his office and tucked her blouse more deeply into her skirt, a maneuver she had practiced at home with revealing results, and he actually stared up at the ceiling above his desk.

Bill had no such qualms. He neither stared nor turned away from what was being offered for his contemplation; he simply looked, with the same kind of indifferent curiosity that he had been bestowing on the thing in his hand.

"What is it?" Catherine asked.

"Beats me," he said. "It's called a Big Guzzler, but what exactly it guzzles or to what end, totally escapes me. And I think the instructions were originally written in Japanese. Do you suppose 'tul' means 'turn' or 'pull'?"

Catherine took it from his hand, and holding it in front of her she tried in her imagination to fit it somewhere in or on her body. Without success. She handed it back and sat down.

"Feeling better?" he asked.

"Much."

"Come in to buy something?"

"It's embarrassing, but I'm not sure I know how any of them works."

He looked at her intently.

"I don't know how all of them work either. The fun is finding out."

She turned restlessly in her chair.

"Do you have a cigarette?" she asked.

"I'll get one," he said.

He went out into the store and came back with a pack of cigarettes. He offered one to her, which she took, and matches. But when she tried to light it, her hand was shaking violently.

"Why don't you just tell me," he said after he had lit her cigarette.

She watched the smoke curl up from the end of the cigarette.

"I want a man."

There was a sudden gush of warmth between her legs.

He did not appear surprised.

"Where?" he said.

"Here. But I want him blindfolded."

"Carol," he smiled, "you've got it a little mixed up, I think. It's you who's blindfolded. You don't want him to recognize you, is that it?"

"Yes, I suppose so," she said quietly.

"For him to see, but not you."

I don't know. I don't know what I want."

"I think I do," he said. "It's not so strange, after all, though it may be to you. Like everyone else, you want to step out of your skin and have somebody else's experience, without the inhibitions and the fears and the guilt. To be somebody else for just a little while and then step back into yourself as if nothing had happened. And it's probably the most desirable, and the most fun, with sex because it's the most taboo."

"I'm not looking for fun," she said.

He sat looking at her for a very long time.

"This is not exactly a housewife's lark, is it?" he said at last.

She looked down at the gold band on her finger. She had meant to remove it.

"How do I know I can trust you?" she asked.

He shrugged and picked up the pink plastic again.

"Trust is a little irrelevant at this point, Carol. You want this very badly and I can get it for you. In the end you'll convince yourself that you trust me."

"I wish I could believe you."

"You will, I assure you. And if you don't, you just won't come back. It's that simple."

Yes, she supposed it was. He went back to his Japanese instructions. She lit another cigarette, more calmly this time.

"How does it work?" she said at last. "This arrangement."

"When you get more interested, I'll tell you how it works. You've got to decide first, that's all."

"You're leading me on, aren't you?"

"Of course I'm leading you on." He turned back to her. "You want this very much, I can tell. But you also want someone to take you there, to persuade you. Well, I'm not exactly a stranger to your need, so I'll take you."

"Am I supposed to ask you what your need is?" she smiled. Her courage was returning.

"I don't imagine you could fill it," he said evenly.

"Why? Are you gay?"

"No, Carol, straight as the proverbial arrow. I get off on torts. I'm a lawyer."

"How about tarts?" she smiled again.

"Only of a very special kind," he smiled in return.

"So why aren't you practicing law instead of sitting here with a Japanese machine-gun in your hands?"

"Is *that* what it is?" he said, looking at the thing in his hands. "Simple. I was disbarred."

"I'm sorry."

118

"It's all right," he said unconcernedly. "They're getting along without me. Maybe even better."

She got up and put on her jacket.

"Well, I'm going," she said. "And I'll think about it, whether to trust a disbarred lawyer and a kid who reads Kipling."

"Don't worry, Dean is not part of the deal. Hang on, I'll go with you. I've put together enough toys for today."

"You don't seem very impressed by the stuff in here," she said, gazing around the room.

"Oh, some of it is all right," he said as he collected various pieces of pink plastic and returned them to their boxes. "But most of it is junk. People stroll by, very blasé and very up-tight people, they force themselves inside, buy a gadget. They take it home, give it a pop and a laugh and then throw it into the closet for their kids to discover. A little mechanical slumming in Sin City. I told you, like you I'm into obsession, and you don't need toys for that. Just the old fucked-up head God gave you and something to bang it against."

"You sound like my doctor," she said.

"Why, was he disbarred too?"

"Not yet."

They stood in the twilight outside the shop.

"Bill, I've decided. You're right. I want it and I'll do whatever you say."

He looked at her briefly, then took out his wallet and extracted a business card with a name, Giorgio di Martina, and a phone number at an East Side address.

"Call this number anytime in the afternoon and they'll make an appointment."

"An appointment? I thought here."

"No, not here. There," he said, pointing to the card in her hand. "It's better this way. Trust me," he smiled.

"Bill, am I going to have to pay for this?"

"No, Carol, this one is on me."

He nodded and walked hastily down Sixth Avenue. She watched him briefly then turned and started up toward Twenty-ninth Street and home.

Tom was on the phone when she opened the door, but he hurriedly hung up as soon as she took off her jacket and came into the living room. Maddy, she thought. She went over and kissed him on the cheek. He took her hand and held it. Their moods for once were in harmony. But only briefly. He dropped her hand and drew away from her.

"My God, Catherine, what are you wearing?"

She had forgotten about her nipples poking through the blouse. He stood staring at her.

"What are you trying to do, get raped?"

An angry flush came to her cheeks. And a tingling along her scalp.

"Did it ever occur to you that I might be wearing this for you?"

No, it had not, nor had it occurred to her until that very moment. She suddenly grew fearful that he might accept her suggestion at face value and act upon it. She turned quickly and went into the bathroom and closed the door.

Tom stood looking out the window. Was she dressed this way for him or was his first impulse correct? The smell of cunt. Had he too gotten a whiff? "And it ain't gonna be with you, big boy, nohow."

When Catherine reemerged from the bathroom she was wearing slacks and a bulky knit sweater. She went into the kitchen and Tom followed her.

"Where were you?" he asked.

"In the Village. Shopping."

He had no reason to doubt it, but suddenly he doubted everything.

They stood staring at one another in the kitchen, each daring the other to make the first move, whether a remark or an

120

accusation. Finally Catherine turned away and started preparing dinner. He stood watching her a while, then went to her, turned her toward him and took her in his arms.

"Catherine, I love you."

He kissed her lightly on the mouth. He didn't want to frighten her off this time. And she accepted his kiss as the token it was intended to be. She rested her head on his shoulder.

"I haven't been a very good wife, have I?"

What she really wanted to say, but didn't dare, was that she really didn't care whether he found his sex elsewhere. But that would force him to deny or defend himself, neither of which she wanted to hear. She didn't think he loved Maddy, and if he wanted to make Maddy Kirsch his whore, that was all right.

"I've no complaints," he said.

Oh Tom, you should have, she thought. Many of them.

"Do you ever wish you weren't married?" she asked.

"No, of course not."

She didn't know whether she did or not. It was probably better this way. It shielded her from other men and their terrible and persistent claims on her. It would be horrible to be single again. The pressure to date, to go out or, in their vile phrase, to put out. She didn't know if she truly loved her husband, but she did know she was grateful to him for suffering her.

It was a pity he couldn't save her as well, she thought sadly.

Her head was still upon his shoulder.

"Would you prefer I didn't wear that bra?"

An invitation. An appeal. A cry.

He raised her head and looked into her tear-filled eyes. Had he really made her so unhappy?

"If you like it, then wear it. Just be careful, Catherine."

Yes, she thought sadly. I'll be careful.

His own thoughts echoed only Maddy's sarcasm. "I'll take precautions. My bed or hers?"

He kissed her again and turned away to hide his own tears.

Twelve

The di Martina house—she had no other way of thinking of it— was an elegant but unobtrusive brownstone on East Sixty-third between First and Second Avenues, and Catherine arrived at the door precisely at three.

She had left the Council at lunchtime, with a message to Mr. Gillespie that she was not feeling well and would not return. She walked home as usual, took a bath and shaved her legs. She put on her Bloomingdale's underwear, hesitated briefly over the lipstick, but in the end just dropped it in a small nylon tote. She put fifty dollars in the bag as well, but removed her wallet, credit cards, address and check books. She took her latchkey off its ring and that too went into the tote. She slipped off her wedding band and put it under her pillow. The other things, her formal identity, went into the night table next to her bed. She stopped in the drugstore on the corner, bought a pack of cigarettes and then took a cab to East Sixty-third Street.

A man answered the door. He was short and was wearing dark trousers, white shirt and tie, but no jacket. He looks like an accountant, she thought.

"Mr. di Martina?"

"No, Mr. di Martina isn't here right now."

"I'm Carol. I have an appointment at three."

He stood aside to let her enter and then said simply, "Upstairs."

She passed under the crystal chandelier in the entry hall and went before him up the deeply carpeted stairs. She could feel his eyes on her legs behind her. Was he the one?

"Here," he said and opened the door to one of the rooms on the second floor.

"Thank you," she said and went in. The door closed behind her and the man with the white shirt and tie was gone.

The room looked like an ordinary bedroom, a little old-fashioned perhaps, but bright and airy and clean. She looked at the poster bed, picked up the edge of the white cotton coverlet. Clean sheets. There was a dresser, an armchair near the window and a straight-backed chair by the bed. She opened the closet. Empty. She put her tote on the bed and sat uneasily on its edge.

She was startled by the loud ring of the phone on the night table next to the bed. It rang once, twice, three times before she decided to pick it up.

"Hello," she said, feeling a little foolish.

"There's a blindfold under the pillow," the voice said. "Place the wooden chair with its back to the door. Put on the blindfold and sit on the chair with your hands behind your back."

Catherine did as she was told. She had a momentary sense of panic when she tied on the blindfold, but she calmed herself. She sat listening to her own heartbeat, feeling it in her temples where the white cloth of the blindfold pressed in upon them.

What was she doing here? she suddenly thought. She had not imagined or wanted it this way. All at once all the repressed fear exploded inside her. She was disoriented and terrified by her own boldness and by the uncharted and, as she now realized, the uncontrollable course that lay like a blind path before her. She abruptly snatched off the blindfold and ran out into the hall. Bill was coming up the stairs, a large leather case in his hand. There was no other way out. She bolted down the stairs, pushed past him and down into the foyer. He turned and watched her without movement and without expression as she unlocked the front door and ran out into the sunlight.

Catherine half walked and half ran to the corner of Second Avenue and was about to hail a cab when she realized that she had left her bag with the money in the room. She looked at her watch. Three-thirty. She could walk to the Council. She cast a cautious glance back down Sixty-third Street. No one.

Catherine walked over to Third Avenue and then turned and started downtown. After a couple of blocks a sudden nausea rose into her throat. She was afraid she would throw up on the street, and her embarrassment forced her into a bar on the corner of Fifty-fifth. The bartender mercifully signalled the ladies' room with his eyes. She walked quietly to the rear, went in and vomited into the toilet. She cleaned it up as best she could and left, her eyes carefully averted from the bartender's curious stare.

She felt better with the knot of fear and anxiety out of her stomach. My God, she silently groaned, what was I about to let myself in for? The thought suddenly occurred to her that it was Bill who was going to use her for his "obsession," whatever that was. He had almost trapped her by his apparent indifference. She tried to figure it out. She would be tied to the chair, she guessed. Then what? Would he use one of his "toys"? What was in the leather case? She shuddered with chill in the warm sunlight. No, that's not the way it should be, not that way at all. Her pace slowed.

On the opposite corner of Forty-sixth across Third Avenue two women were standing and having an animated conversation.

One of them, the black one, was dressed in a short leather skirt and boots and what appeared to Catherine across the street like a blond wig. Her companion had long straight black hair like Catherine's and was wearing a beige suit, the tight skirt slit deeply up the thigh. It was the long black hair that first caught Catherine's eye, and now she stood and watched the two of them laughing and gesturing on the other side of Third Avenue.

Are they whores, she wondered. The black girl certainly looked like one, but what about the other? She couldn't tell. The white girl with the black hair had turned and was now facing her. Catherine moved back to the building line, out of the way of the sidewalk traffic. The black-haired girl was wearing a peach blouse like Catherine's own, she could now see, and it was open to mid-breast. Catherine unconsciously put her hand up to the buttons of her own blouse.

By now they had seen her as well. There was a brief, more private conversation on the sidewalk opposite, and when the light turned green, they quickly crossed over to her side of the street. Catherine did not move.

"Why don't you get your fancy titties out of here," the black girl said.

Catherine looked at her. She was stunningly beautiful under the heavy makeup and the silver eye shadow. Catherine wondered why she bothered, with a face like that.

"Come on, move it," her companion said.

"I was just standing here," Catherine said.

"That's just the point, honey. *Don't* stand here," the black girl said with an almost indifferent air that undercut her apparent anger.

"She's no hooker, Marvina," the other said after she had finished her close-up inspection of Catherine O'Rourke Donovan, late of Star of the Sea parish in Bayside. "Are you?"

Marvina too checked her out and shrugged. "It still does no good havin' a broad across the street. It's like we're givin' a concert."

"What are you, an amateur?" the other asked.

"I'm married," Catherine said nervously.

They both laughed.

"Terrific ID," Marvina snorted. "Does your old man know you're workin' the streets? Come on, Daisy, let's go up a couple of blocks. This cheesecake looks like she's set in concrete."

Daisy was still studying Catherine.

"You from out of town?" she asked somewhat more mildly.

"No. Here. Queens."

Marvina was already a few steps off and now Daisy turned to join her."

"Wait a minute," Catherine called. Daisy stopped and turned back to her. "Do you want to have a cup of coffee or something? Can I buy you a drink?"

Daisy came back and Marvina stood where she was, hand on hip, and watched.

"What is this?" Daisy demanded. "Are you a social worker or something?"

"Maybe she's from the TV," Marvina called. "Are you from the TV?"

"I'm in trouble. I need to talk," Catherine let tumble out quickly. "I just had a fight with my husband."

"Give us a *break*, will you," Daisy said and started off once again. "Christ, she had a fight with her husband and she wants to discuss it with two hookers on Forty-sixth Street."

"Wait. Please. I'll pay you."

Daisy turned once more. Again the speculative look.

"Well now, why didn't you say that. That's Marvina's department, sweetie. Marvina," Daisy signalled with her head, "you got yourself a customer."

Marvina strolled back to them and cast a long look up and down Catherine's body.

"It'll cost you fifty," she said, "but I'll give you an hour and the time of your life, sugar tits."

126

It began to dawn on Catherine what kind of a deal was being struck.

"I don't have fifty dollars," she said.

"Then try Fourteenth Street," Marvina said matter of factly. "I hear they're givin' it away for nothin' down there."

"Don't you understand. I just want to talk." She paused and forced it out of her throat. "I don't want to get laid."

"Get *her*," Marvina chortled.

Catherine looked down blankly at her hands.

"I don't have any money at all. I left it there."

Daisy glanced at her wristwatch, then at Marvina.

"Come on, Marnie, what the hell, let's buy her a coffee. There's nothing happening here anyway."

Marvina jittered briefly on the pavement then shrugged her agreement.

They went into a coffee shop on Forty-third, Catherine between them, and all three bathed in hot stares. Catherine tried to separate herself, to move a little to the side, but it made no difference: the gentlemen in Aristotle's Coffee Shoppe had wide-angle vision when it came to ladies who charged for it. They sat themselves, Catherine on one side, Daisy and Marvina on the other, in a booth near the window.

"So," Daisy said, shaking her sugar packet loudly, "you had a fight with your husband."

"You're gonna ruin your teeth with that refined shit," said Marvina who waged the holy war against tooth decay always and everywhere. She turned to Catherine. "Are you gonna ask me why I'm a whore, white lady?"

"You were born a whore, Marvina," Daisy volunteered.

"These Greeks aren't much for juke boxes, are they?" Marvina complained as she inspected the premises, absolutely oblivious of the stares that now rested openly and immovably on their table. "Could use some music," she continued, drumming her long fingernails on the tabletop. "Hey," she grinned at

Daisy, "you know what I saw the other day up on Fiftieth? A whore with a box! A fuckin' gigantic box, and it's turned up full blast. Boogie all over the street and she's just standin' there, Miss Real Cool, a little flex in the knees, a little snap in the fingers, but no jivin' around. Ain't that bad?"

Catherine wondered what kind of a box.

"She's crazy," Daisy said. "She gets laughs out of turkeys like you, but what john buys a whore with a box?"

"I don't know," Marvina said slyly. "She sure had some box."

"Marvina, give it a rest, will you." Daisy turned back to Catherine opposite her. "You said you were in trouble. What trouble?"

"I almost let a man do something terrible to me just now in a house on Sixty-third Street."

The other two sat drinking their coffee in silence, uncertain where this was going, but willing to let it go.

"I met him in a pornography store in the Village," Catherine continued. "I think he wanted to tie me up or something."

"How much was he payin'?" Marvina wanted to know.

"Nothing. It was supposed to be for me."

"You're nuts, sister, just plain nuts," Marvina sighed into her coffee. "He was good for a note at least. Maybe two on Sixty-third."

"Why don't you just stay home with your husband?" Daisy said, half in sadness and half in disgust.

"I don't sleep with my husband," Catherine said quietly.

"Whee!" Marvina exclaimed as heads turned. "Give me the streets every time."

"Oh, yeah, and why is that?" Daisy smiled. "Can't he make it?"

"No, it's me. I can't," Catherine said. "I'm afraid."

128

"Well, why don't you go to an agency, or somethin'?" Marvina groaned. "Daisy, we're losin' money sittin' here with this fruitcake."

Catherine looked down into her coffee.

"OK," Daisy intervened, "you're afraid. So what's with this other crap on Sixty-third street. That's a lot more dangerous than screwing your husband."

"I'm not afraid of the danger. They'll never do anything to me."

"Oh won't they?" Daisy said quietly. "That's nice to know. And just what the hell are you up to?"

"I don't know yet. I just want to hurt them. All of them. I want to make them sorry."

"Some guy did some number on you, lady. So what's the big deal," Marvina said shaking her head.

Catherine looked first at one and then at the other.

"Don't you hate men? With what they do to you?"

"You mean like payin' the bills?" Marvina said. "Screw that other shit. You give me the green, my man, and I love you. Now. Forever. Maybe even for a whole week."

"Sure," Daisy said in a voice that was scarcely audible. "Sure."

Marvina brightened with a new recollection.

"You know who really had it for guys? Daisy, do you remember that whore Bonnie who used to cut up her tricks? She had nails the size of a carvin' knife, and while they were gettin' off she took about eight yards of nice white skin off their backs. They loved it while she was doin' it, but afterwards they couldn't move for a month. But some fuckin' trick went and died of blood poisonin' and they chased her off the streets. She lives in Jersey now, Hoboken or someplace."

"That's not exactly what you had in mind, was it?" Daisy said to Catherine. "By the way, what's your name?"

"Carol."

"Yeah. Well I'm Daisy and this overdone turkey is Marvina."

"Marvina," Catherine said, "you know you're very beautiful. It struck me the first time I saw you. I mean it."

"Why, thank you," Marvina said with genuine gratitude. "It's nice of you to say that."

"And you, Daisy, I thought looked like me."

"Don't I wish," Daisy smiled. "If I did, I'd be rich. With your body you could probably make a million out here. But not on the corner of Forty-third and Third. Upstairs, in an apartment."

"Oh *yeah*," Marvina gurgled, "an apartment. A little personal pad over on Park."

"Or the brownstone I was in on Sixty-third," Catherine reflected. "That wasn't bad either."

"No, forget the hash dreams," Daisy said sourly. "This life sucks. Stick with your husband. Fuckin' or not, it's better than this.".

"You nuts, Daisy?" Marvina cried. "We're talkin' about walkin' around money. Your old man work, lady?"

"Yes, of course."

"There you go," Marvina said. "You do a little daytime hustle and you're still home in time to have supper on the table."

"I have a job too, a good one," Catherine said.

"Yeah, well." Marvina drooped noticeably. "You don't want to lose that. Maybe you could hustle in the office," she added without any real enthusiasm. The Park Avenue apartment was receding into the remote distance.

"I thought you were afraid?" Daisy asked.

"I am," Catherine confessed. "I guess I'm just fantasizing."

Daisy sat staring at Catherine over her coffee. At last she looked at her watch. "Time to go," she announced. "Marvina, this is yours." She passed her the check.

"Shit," Marvina said, "money don't grow on trees." But she got up nonetheless and went over to the cashier.

There was a sudden silence across the table.

"So?" Daisy said at last.

"I don't know. I'm sorry I wasted your time. Made you lose money. I was just so frightened. Then I saw you standing there, and it was like seeing myself."

"I'm nothing like you. I'd make book on it."

"Maybe not," Catherine said slowly. "Maybe I'm like you."

Another silence, this time punctuated by the rhythmic and nervous tattoo of Daisy's nails on the formica tabletop.

"What do you want from me?" Daisy asked. The nervousness was now in her throat as well.

"I don't know. Something. I'll pay you."

Daisy glanced toward Marvina chatting busily at the cash register.

"What the hell," she said at last. "I've got to go, but here, take my number."

Daisy wrote her number on a piece of napkin with her eyebrow pencil and slid it across the table to Catherine. Catherine tore off another piece, took the pencil from Daisy's hand, and wrote her own number on it.

"Here's mine," she said. "The bottom one's work. It's just down the street, as a matter of fact. Thirty-ninth."

Marvina returned.

"I got a deal from the cashier. No charge for the coffee if we don't come back ever, ever, *ever* again. Sound good to you guys?"

The other two stood up.

"Nice to have met you," Catherine said.

"Yeah," said Daisy and extended her hand.

"Sure," chimed Marvina. "Any time you got nothing to do. And give our best to your old man, you hear?"

With a wave Catherine turned and went south on Third Avenue. The other two watched her as she disappeared in the crowd.

"Your pal is a real space cadet," Marvina said.

"Sure," Daisy said reflectively. "Maybe."

Catherine now lay on Neil Astrakhan's couch as a matter of course, and the gush of recollection and association was swifter and deeper.

I went into Gillespie's office and stood in front of him. He was dressed like a priest but it was Gillespie all right. I stood there and slowly raised my skirt. I had no pants on. He had a heart attack and he died.

I was trapped by a sailor in a large house uptown. He caught me and tied me to a chair. He waved his cock at me and tried to hit me with it. I bit it off and spit it out. I bit off the ropes and escaped.

I met two whores on the street, one black and one white. The black one wanted to fuck me but the other one wouldn't let her. The white one took off her wig and it was my mother. I promised I would never ever, *ever* go there again. He said there was no charge.

"Who's Gillespie?" Neil Astrakhan asked.

"The man I work for at the Council. Why?"

"It's the first name you've mentioned."

"I didn't mention his name."

Thirteen

"Who's the girl?"

Grace was sitting in Tom Donovan's office, in the selfsame seat lately warmed by the smaller but somewhat more muscled bottom of Maddy Kirsch. The door was closed behind her, as was her privilege, and her red spiked heels were propped up on his desk.

"What girl?" he asked as he shuffled pointlessly through a number of long defunct personnel files.

"You know the girl I mean, Tomas. The skinny one with the blond curls who was in here with you."

"Oh *that* girl. Just a girl."

"Does that mean you're going to stop coming around to see me?"

Grace's interest in his answer seemed half-hearted at best since she was presently entertaining herself by going through her co-workers' personnel files on his desk. He could save her the trouble, Tom thought. Cindy Rehder had no private life worth bothering about. And Grace had very nice legs and thighs, he noticed for the tenth time since she put them up on the desk for his inspection.

"You know," he said, "when I was growing up all the guys in my neighborhood said that Puerto Rican girls were hot. Do you think they're hot, Gracie?"

"I'm *very* hot, Tomas," she said without interrupting her reading of Cindy Rehder's turgid biography. "Don't you think so?"

"Yes, *very* hot," he said.

She put down the folder.

"Hotter than your wife?"

"What do you think, Grace, that you plunge a stiletto through my heart every time you mention Catherine? Of course you're hotter than her. If you weren't I'd be sleeping with her and you I'd have posted down to the machine shop."

She tried her best to figure out the logic of that but soon dismissed it as hopeless.

"Am I better than Curlylocks?"

She had at least grasped the principle.

"Now that's an interesting question," he said. "I guess I'd have to see the two of you perform side by side."

"Forget it, Tomas. None of that dirty stuff."

"OK, you suggest something."

"Take me to a movie."

"Can we do the dirty stuff afterwards?"

"You betcha," she grinned and removed her feet from his desk.

"Pick out a movie then, Gracie, an early one, and I'll take care of the rest."

She went to the door, then turned.

"What 'rest'?"

"Curlylocks. She loves movies too."

134

"You got some jokes," she said and left. Not without a small minatory flip of her behind, of course.

There would be no movie, he knew. They never yet had made it as far as the movie.

He picked up the phone and dialed Catherine at the Council.

"How's it going?" he said.

"Like always, I guess. You going to be late tonight again?"

"Yeah. The usual. And you? You OK for dinner?"

"Yes. I was thinking maybe I'll have a friend over."

A friend? Catherine Donovan had no friends, none who came to the house certainly, except Maddy Kirsch, and that didn't seem very likely.

"What friend?"

"Somebody I met last week. She's very nice."

"From the office?"

"No, but she works near here."

"OK. Enjoy. See you later."

A friend? Catherine Donovan had no friends. Not the Catherine Donovan he knew.

He met Grace downstairs in the terminal at five-fifteen. She was reading a pamphlet in Spanish.

"What's that?" he asked.

"Somebody handed it to me. I must look Spanish. It says the church has too much power and should be nationalized."

"Nationalized? What church?"

"La Prima Iglesia Evangélica y Espiritista de Ponce," she read.

"Christ, and I thought they disappeared with the Albigensians and Buffy Sainte-Marie. I've really got to keep up. What movie did you pick?"

"It's religious, I think. *Heaven's Gate*. I love religious movies."

"Perfect. Let's go," he said as he took her arm.

"Don't you want to know where it's playing?"

Grace was a traditionalist. She insisted on observing the forms.

"It's OK. I'll find it."

They went outside.

"Taxi!"

Grace hopped in and Tom followed.

"Just drive up Eighth Avenue," he instructed the driver. "I'll let you know."

He gently slid his hand under Grace's thin dress, eyes casually out the window.

"Lovely night," he said looking benignly at the human debris along Eighth Avenue.

He found what he was looking for under her dress. Slowly she melted toward him. By Columbus Circle they were all but horizontal on the rear seat.

At Seventieth and Central Park West he raised his head.

"Take the Eighty-sixth Street transverse," he commanded. "Lex and Ninety-sixth."

"Tomas," she said, "come back here."

She was hot all right. Just like the guys in the neighborhood said.

Catherine thought she would try to find Daisy on Forty-sixth Street during her lunch hour, but she tried the number first, just in case.

"Hello."

"I woke you up, didn't I? I'm sorry," Catherine apologized.

"Of course you woke me up. Who is this?"

"Catherine. Carol. You remember, we met last week on the street. We had coffee. With Marvina."

"Oh yeah. Sure. What's up?"

"I'm really sorry about waking you up, Daisy."

"It's OK. OK."

"I was wondering if you'd like to come down here and have dinner with me tonight. Just the two of us. My husband will be out."

136

There was a long pause on the other end of the line.

"What time?" Daisy asked at last.

"Well, I could meet you at five and we could walk home together."

"Carol, sweetheart, I don't work in an office. If I leave off working at five, I'm dead. And so are the commuters."

"How about seven or seven-thirty then?"

"Christ, you're going to bankrupt me, lady. Oh, the hell with it. I'll work a double shift on the weekend."

"You work *shifts*?" Catherine exclaimed.

"Relax. It's just a way of talking. Seven-thirty is better. Where do you live?"

"The apartment house on the corner of Twenty-ninth and Lexington. 15M. Donovan."

"Donovan, that's nice. Sounds domestic. How does Daisy Plimpton sound?"

"Classy."

"It should," Daisy Plimpton said. "I made it up myself."

Daisy arrived at seven forty-five. Even Catherine could tell that she had first gone home, or somewhere, and changed. The heavy makeup was gone, the golden chains, the sky-high slit skirt stretched so tight across her bottom that you could see the cleft between her buttocks. Miss Plimpton, younger now, but somewhat more worn, was dressed in jeans, a purple sweater and fuchsia moccasins.

"I thought your husband might be home after all," she explained, "and I didn't want him to get a hard-on."

Catherine displayed a small frown.

"I'm sorry," Daisy said quickly. "I didn't mean to offend you by talking that way about your husband. But you said you didn't sleep with him and I thought, well. . ."

"No, it's not that," Catherine said. "There are just some words I can't get used to. Like the one you used. Sometimes I think I'm even going to faint when I hear them. Why do people have to talk that way?"

137

"I don't know," Daisy said helplessly. "They just talk that way."

"Do you want a drink, Daisy?"

They took their drinks and sat at the kitchen table.

"Very nice," Daisy said as she inspected the kitchen. "Where does your husband work?"

"In the Port Authority Terminal."

"In the PA! My God, I used to work there."

"You worked in the PA? Really?"

She caught Daisy's ambiguous smile.

"Oh, I see what you mean," Catherine said. "How dumb I am sometimes. But what a terrible place to work, especially for a, a. . ."

"A whore? Is that another of your words?"

"Sorry."

"Well, that's one you're going to have to get over if we're ever going to talk. Come on, try it. It's just a word. Five times and you'll be over it. Like hiccups."

"Whore. Whore. Whore. Whore. Whore," Catherine repeated.

"There you go," Daisy said. "Nothing to it. I am a whore, you are a whore, she is a whore. Just like in school."

"I am a whore. You are a whore."

Catherine rose quickly and retrieved two ramekins of shrimp in marinara sauce from the oven.

"See, I told you," Daisy said encouragingly. "Easy as pie. Yeah, well getting back to the PA, it was no picnic but in this racket you've got to start somewhere, and that's as good a place as any, I guess, especially if you have no connections. I tried to work commuters mostly and stay away from the human garbage. The trouble is, you have to make it right there. I gave so many blowjobs in the PA that my mouth. . ."

Catherine's hand began to tremble as she was ladling rice onto Daisy's plate.

"Oh God, is that another one?" Daisy asked uneasily. "Maybe I should just shut up."

Catherine slowly replaced the rice pot on the stove. She stood there, hands on the edge of the stove, her eyes fixed directly on the blank wall in front of her.

"Yes," she said as she turned back to the table, "that's another one. But please don't make me say that one five times, Daisy. And please don't leave."

"OK," she said, "OK, easy does it." She turned sideways in her chair and appeared to study the yellowed recipes taped to the cabinet beside her. "You know, Marvina was right. Somebody really did a number on you, Carol. Do you know who? Was it some priest? Your father? It's usually your father."

"No," Catherine said quietly. "It wasn't my father. And please eat."

"Well, it was mine," Daisy said matter-of-factly. "He had me when I was thirteen. In good old Somerville, Mass."

A long dark shadow passed across Catherine's face. There was a taste of bitter, briny water on her tongue.

"Aren't you terribly angry about it, Daisy? How can you sit there and talk so calmly about it?"

"No point in getting riled up'now. He's long gone. Cancer, my mother says. Clap, I say. Take your pick, Carol."

"Daisy, Carol isn't my real name. It's Catherine. I'm sorry I lied about that."

"It's all right. We all have more than one name. And Catherine's very nice. Kind of an old-fashioned name."

"Daisy?"

Daisy looked up from her tally of the shrimp left in the marinara.

"Yeah?"

"Daisy, I want you to take me with you one day."

"Take you with me? Where?"

"On your job."

Daisy slammed her fork down on the table.

"Look, Catherine or Carol or whatever the hell your name is, don't jerk me around like I'm stupid. I don't like what I do for a living. In fact, I hate it. It's disgusting and degrading. But I have to do it because I'm fucked up and it's the only thing I can do and yeah, I'm very used to the money. But don't come around and pretend it's some kind of exciting game, because it isn't. If you want to go slumming, try something else. Try getting arrested, why don't you, and try playing at jail. Well, I've been in jail like every other whore in this city, and that's no fun either. No, on second thought, why don't you go fuck yourself, since you don't seem to be able to fuck your old man. You're the *real* whore, baby."

"I don't deny that, Daisy. I'm the real whore, as you say. But not for money."

"No," Daisy said, "for kicks. That's what makes you worse than me."

"No, not for kicks either."

Catherine reached out and put her hand on Daisy's.

"I don't know if I can explain this to you, Daisy. I can't even explain it to myself."

"So why don't you see a doctor then?" Daisy said as she slowly descended from her angry explosion.

"I do. He can't help me."

Daisy's anger began to be displaced by a cautious sympathy.

"You really can't make it with your husband?"

"No, I hate sex. And I'm afraid of it."

"You sure think a lot about it."

"I guess I do," Catherine said sadly.

"You hate sex and you want me to take you with me? Why do you need me? Why not go downstairs and give yourself away to the first john you meet?"

"You don't understand, Daisy. I don't want to give myself at all."

140

"Oh, so *that's* it," Daisy said with a brightening under-standing. "You want to work a little stunt. Like rub their faces in it."

"That's it. And not just rub. Grind," Catherine said quietly.

Daisy regarded the dark woman across the table.

"Lady, you are not a kind person."

"You think not?" she said without expression. "I don't."

"And besides, it's dangerous. You get caught out and you're in big trouble, Miss Nipples." Daisy had another sudden en-lightenment. "Yes, my God, you've already started your little game, haven't you? The tits. And the porn store. You little bitch, you're cruising them already."

Catherine got up and poured them both another glass of wine.

"I need you, Daisy. I don't really have the nerve. It *is* dan-gerous and I'm scared."

"Thank God for that. They cut your ears, you know, and other places I won't name because you wouldn't like those words *at all*."

"Who cuts your ears?" Catherine asked, suddenly alarmed.

"The mean customers. And there are lots of them around. Maybe like your friend on Sixty-third Street."

"Bill? My God!"

"I'll bet he was a very calm type, right? Very cool and under control."

"Yes. Exactly."

"That's the type. White Anglo-Saxon sons of bitches. The other dudes just shoot off their mouths a lot, but watch out for those Super Whiteys."

"So, what do I do, Daisy?"

"What do you want to do?"

"I don't know. It's never been altogether real until tonight. Just a kind of idea."

"That's a lot of crap, Catherine. You've probably been playing the scene in your head for years, haven't you?"

141

Catherine nodded without looking up.

"OK, then," Daisy said, draining her glass, "tell me about it and we'll see if we can make your fantasy fly."

Precisely sixty-seven city blocks to the north, on the very same axis of Lexington Avenue, Grace had her dark locks buried in their accustomed place in the crook of Tom Donovan's arm.

"Tom, am I too straight for you?"

He looked down into the dark eyes glinting behind her slowly blinking lashes.

"Gracie, if I could get rid of as many sexual inhibitions as you have, it would be the biggest miracle since Lourdes. No, bigger. The '69 Mets."

"But you always make those jokes. First you want to pay me. Then you want Curlylocks and me together."

"Just jokes."

"I don't know about men's jokes," she said doubtfully. "They always turn out to be serious."

"Don't you understand, Grace? Men float their fantasies in front of women like trial balloons. They expect to have them shot down. So just fire away. Nobody will get hurt," he assured her. "Don't you have any fantasies?"

Grace murmured and turned over on her stomach.

"We've *done* that," he said with elaborate patience. "I mean something you've never even dared do."

She turned over again.

"Well," she began hesitantly. "Sometimes I wonder what it would be like to go down to the terminal and give myself to somebody."

"For nothing?"

"No," she conceded. "For money."

"I wonder if sex has to be dangerous to be really good?" he mused.

She snuggled up closer to his arm.

"Is it dangerous with Curlylocks?"

142

"No," he laughed. "Not really, not as long as you're in good shape."

"Tom!" She suddenly sat upright in bed. "I know what."

"What?"

"Let's do it in the PA! You and me. We'll pretend. I'll pick you up, we'll do it and you can pay me. Please! Say you'll do it."

He thought about it, not very clearly perhaps since he could see her dark shining eyes fixed upon him in the flickering light of the votive candle on the dresser.

"All right, Gracie. We'll pretend," he said. "We'll do it. Tomorrow."

"*Fantástico!*"

Fourteen

"Catherine, I really don't think the Port Authority is a good idea," Daisy said. "It's filled with cops, for one thing, and with some very tough trade. And why the hell do you want to do this in a place where your husband works?"

Catherine stood in front of her bathroom mirror and inspected herself.

"It'll do," Daisy said from behind her. "Enough to send the message but not enough of a message to send you to the slammer."

"Do they really put people in jail for this?"

"No, not usually," Daisy sighed. "Not unless you make the mistake of soliciting a cop or try to fuck on top of the Trailways counter."

Catherine gave herself another careful look. Her reflection in the mirror made her a little self-conscious, but it wasn't as bad

144

as she had imagined: she thought she would look in the glass and see some pale and mitigated version of Marvina.

Daisy had done the make-up, had applied the shiny red lipstick, the eye-liner and blue shadow that she now wore. The heels were exactly too high and the skirt exactly too short—Catherine vetoed the hip-high slit—and her blouse was open to a point that could have been construed as either deliberate suggestion or simple carelessness. And the nipples, well. The total effect was not a lubricious bulletin and it was not exactly a letter home. Somewhere in between. A mailgram perhaps. Here I am, it said. Maybe.

"I can't handle the street, Daisy. It's, I don't know, too public, too exposed. And a bar or someplace like that is too confining. I'd feel trapped and I'm afraid I'd panic."

"And your husband? He works upstairs from the terminal, doesn't he?"

"Yes, but he never goes down there during the day, I'm sure. It's like a different world up there in those offices."

"Well, I hope so," Daisy said. "Now, let's make sure you got it straight. If I signal 'no,' then it's absolutely positively 'no.' Remember, you have no instincts and I don't want you to make a wrong move. Are you hearing me, Catherine? This is dangerous."

"You do it every day, Daisy. It can't be that dangerous."

"I know what I'm doing; you don't. And worse, you've got something else up your sleeve, lady. You're like an arsonist joining the fire department and *that's* what's making me nervous."

"I'll be all right," Catherine said with just a suggestion of annoyance.

"Well, I'll be there. And remember, do *not*, for any reason, leave with anybody. You promise?"

"Yes, mommy, I promise. Please, let's go."

They went, Daisy with a final long sigh, Catherine with rising excitement and fear, which she tried her best not to show to Daisy. Daisy had decided that three o'clock would probably be the best time, and though she didn't describe him to Catherine, she had the target type already picked out. A businessman, somebody in a suit anyway, with one or two drinks from lunch under his belt and a bulge in his pants once he got back to the office. A little restlessness, the jacket back on and into the Port Authority to find sweet, sexy Catherine Donovan. Without even knowing him, Daisy had imagined Mr. Eugene Gillespie.

"Upper level," Daisy commanded. "Jersey buses."

They took the elevator up to the esplanade level and turned into the waiting area, an arcade that overlooked the ground floor promenade.

"OK now," Daisy said. "Sit over there, your back to the downstairs level. I'll be right here," pointing to the head of the escalators, "and sit so you can see me and I can see you." She looked at Catherine. "You going to be all right?"

"I think so."

"Terrific. She thinks so. Well, go ahead. And do just what I told you."

Catherine was a little uncertain on the high heels, but she navigated one very slow circuit through the waiting area without mishap. It was only about one-third full at that hour, fifteen or twenty people, some looking into space, some reading, others trying to manage children. And all somehow now aware of the new presence of Catherine Donovan.

As she walked slowly along the rows on chairs she could feel her face growing hot under their stares. She was aware that eyes were following her, whose or how many she did not know, but she could feel them upon her, sniffing, prying into her. She glanced quickly to see if Daisy was there. She was. Her hand went up to the buttons on her blouse.

Daisy watched her from across the room and realized that for the first time in her life she was seeing herself. Catherine was right: there was a distinct resemblance, she now conceded, maybe because of the clothes and the makeup. No, more. The look. The way she held herself, the way she moved. She watched her other self parading, offering. It was a curious feeling, she thought, being inside and outside yourself, seeing Catherine Donovan as others must see Daisy Plimpton. She was not entirely displeased. You've got somehow to believe in yourself to do that, she reflected. Hey, here I am. I'm attractive and I'm desirable. I've got what you want, what everybody wants, and it's worthwhile enough that you're going to pay for it. I'm not giving it away, Jack. It'll cost, that lovely thing you crave.

Catherine picked out her green plastic chair and sat down. There were empty seats on both sides of her and she was facing the entry to the waiting area. She crossed her legs, hitched her skirt a little higher. She took a cigarette out of her handbag. She smoked, and as she did she swept the scene in front of her, not concentrating on anyone or anything, but with a kind of open, curious, bored glance. Unoccupied and available. Maybe.

It didn't take long. A young man facing her from about three rows away got up and walked around and past her, inspecting her furtively out of the corner of his eye. He's frightened, she smiled to herself, more frightened than I am. He came around once again and sat down in a seat directly opposite her. He was not much older than she was, maybe even younger, wearing jeans and an alligator shirt. She uncrossed her legs and he watched, not openly she noticed, but on the oblique. She grew impatient. She took another cigarette from her bag, looked up at him and said, "Got any matches?"

"I don't smoke," he said from his chair opposite.

Serves me right, she thought. My own line. She took out her own matches.

He got up and came over and sat next to her.

Catherine glanced over at Daisy, who shrugged. Who knows? Try it.

"Where you going, Miss?"

"Nowhere."

"Just sitting," he smiled pleasantly.

"Just sitting," she smiled back. "What's on your mind?"

"Nothing. I'm going to Metuchen."

She just sat and looked at him, trying very hard not to laugh.

"Then why don't you go," she said at last. "Fuck off, kid." Just to see what it would feel like.

The young man abruptly rose from his seat and left, possibly for the bus to Metuchen.

The sudden, crude, unexpected and unprovoked blow felt marvelous. She smiled across the room at Daisy and Daisy smiled back.

Catherine resumed her sweep. She grew impatient again and got up and did another turn around the waiting area. This time she was no longer even aware of the stares.

Back to her seat. Another cigarette. Something had changed. Standing leaning against a railing to her left was now a dark young woman in a black dress and red shoes. She had one leg bent back up on the lower railing behind her and her dress had parted at the side to reveal what seemed to be two or three yards of full, black-stockinged leg. She had curly black hair and a face as carefully painted as Catherine's own.

My God, Catherine thought, a whore!

She looked over at Daisy, but Daisy, assured that Catherine was alone, was thoughtfully checking out the promenade below in that careful observant way that four years of practice had taught her.

The other woman looked at Catherine. Briefly their eyes met and the other looked away.

Daisy was still otherwise occupied.

Catherine got up and went over to the woman in the black dress.

"Look, lady," she said, "I want you out of here, and fast."

The other looked at her with what Catherine could recognize was fear in her eyes.

"I was just standing here," she said nervously.

"That's the point, honey. *Don't*. Do your whoring somewhere else."

The other moved. Fast.

"*Puta*," she hissed with a grin over her shoulder as she left.

Daisy was watching again and smiling.

Catherine walked back to her seat, her hips swinging now. There was a man sitting there.

No, Daisy shook her head. No!

He was a thin man in glasses wearing a suit with a white buttoned shirt but no tie. No, he did not look good even to Catherine. She walked on and sat farther down the same line of seats.

The instincts must not be difficult, Catherine thought. What is difficult is the boredom, the waiting.

"Miss?"

He was standing above and in front of her, blocking Daisy from sight.

"Are you talking to me?" Catherine said evenly.

"Yes. Do you want to come with me?"

He was about forty. Another white shirt, but this time with a tie. His suit jacket was slung over one arm and in his other hand he held a slim leather briefcase.

She didn't need Daisy for this one. Yes.

"Where?" she asked.

"Downstairs."

"Where downstairs?"

"I'll show you."

He's been here before, Catherine thought. Done it before, the pig.

She got up.

Daisy looked him over briefly, nodded. Yes. OK.

They went downstairs to the main terminal promenade, then along one of the side corridors. Daisy followed at a distance.

"Hold on," Catherine said at last. "This is far enough. Let's talk business."

"How much?" he asked.

Very cool, she thought. Very self-possessed. I'm going to enjoy this one.

"Depends. What do you want?"

He seemed a little surprised. Shouldn't she have asked that, she wondered.

"A blow."

"Thirty." Daisy's rates.

"OK. Over there in the hallway. There's a little alcove," he said.

She went with him. He set down his briefcase, put on his jacket and stood with his back against the wall. The hallway was deserted. He started to unzip his fly.

"Not so fast," she said.

He paused, glanced quickly up and down the hall.

"You may be into this mechanical game, cream puff," she said, "but I'm not. And there's not enough money in the world to make me put your filthy cock in my mouth."

"What is this?" he asked in astonishment. And with just a trace of fear.

"This, mister, is your chance of a lifetime. Your lucky day. Look at me."

She was standing immediately before him, about an arm's length away. She took another step backward and slipped her hand down over her crotch.

"No, not at my face, stupid. Down here."

His eyes left her face and were now fixed to where her hand lay.

"It never occurred to you because you never think of such things, of course, but there's nothing down here under this skirt. No panties. Nothing. Just raw hot cunt."

She pressed her fingers slowly into her skirt.

"And it's very wet."

150

It was indeed. She could feel it.

"Would you like to see it?" she asked.

"Yes, I'd very much like to see it," he said in a low voice.

He was perspiring now; there were thick beads of moisture on his forehead and his upper lip.

"It will cost you two hundred."

"What? For a look?"

"You got it. Two notes."

There was a long silence. Somewhere off in the distance water was dripping.

"I don't have two hundred dollars."

"That's really too bad. Really. Then you'd better pick up your little bag, hadn't you, and catch your bus home to mommy because I have other things to do."

He picked up his briefcase.

"I can get it," he said hoarsely.

"See, you've learned something. You've just discovered why the money machine was invented."

His eyes were still upon her hand, and what he imagined lay under it.

"I'll be upstairs for twenty minutes, no more. So move."

He hurried off down the hallway, down past Daisy who was standing leaning against the wall, back into the light and noise of the promenade.

"How did it go?" Daisy asked.

"All right," Catherine said, her eyes gleaming with excitement. "For a start. Let's go have a drink."

"Easy, girl, easy," Daisy said and put her hand on Catherine's still shaking arm.

Outside on the main concourse Grace was on the phone near the Trailways counter.

"Tomas? Yes. Hey, wait a minute. Just hold on."

She turned, phone in hand, and watched Catherine and Daisy walking across the promenade and out the Ninth Avenue exit.

151

"Tomas? You know what? I was chased off the esplanade."

"What? I told you to be careful of the cops."

"No, no, not by a cop. By a whore! Can you imagine it, she thought I was cutting into her turf. What fun!"

Tom laughed on the other end.

"Have you got another spot?" he asked.

"No, it's OK. She's left. I must look terrific. I do look terrific. Same place, Tomas. Give me ten minutes."

"Christ, you sound like a method actor. Got to get into your role. OK. I'll be there in ten minutes."

Grace went back to the esplanade waiting area, looked around quickly and sat down where Catherine had been. Jesus, she thought, she took me for a real whore.

Tom came down and sat across from her. Grace picked up her magazine and pretended to read, her legs crossed so that the slit dress fell away from her thigh. The man without the tie was still in his place, carefully observing the area, and now Grace, through his rimless glasses. He rose, walked past, and then returned and sat down next to her. Grace lowered her magazine and looked at Tom, who sat smiling but unmoving. She raised the magazine again. The tieless man leaned over and said something to her. The magazine fell to her lap. She looked once again beseechingly at Tom, who now got up and crossed over to her.

"Is something wrong, dear?" he asked, looking first at her and then at the man beside her.

"This man said something disgusting to me."

The man without the tie abruptly got up and headed for the escalator. Tom sat down at her side.

"What did he say?" he laughed.

Grace made a face.

"He wanted to know if I'd give him an enema."

"An enema?"

"Yes. What a creep."

"The poor man, he's probably ill and just needed some

medical help," Tom said. "You know, you look pretty sexy, miss. Wanna go fuck?"

"Fuck? Here? What do I look like?" she pouted.

"A whore."

"Oh good," she brightened. "Let's fuck."

"Wait a minute. Aren't you going to tell me how much?"

She thought.

"Ten dollars?"

"This is not San Juan. More."

"OK. Twenty-five."

"Are you very experienced, *señorita?*"

"*Muy perita, señor.*"

"In that case I'll give you thirty."

"I'd do it for nothing, you know that Tomas, don't you?"

"Shut up and take off your clothes."

"Oh no, *señorito*. Not here."

"Where then?"

"Come with me."

She got up and started toward the down escalator. Tom rose and followed at a distance, enjoying her legs, her suggestively undulating hips and behind. He reached the top of the escalator.

"Tom!"

It was Jack Charbonneau coming up.

"Where the hell have you been, Donovan? The comptroller is here."

"Fuck the comptroller."

Grace had stopped at the foot of the escalator and was standing there, hand on hip, looking up at the two men above her.

"Oh, I see," Charbonneau said, glancing down at the promenade. "A little mid-afternoon drinkie with the staff. OK, pal, I'll cover as best I can." His eyes were now back on Grace. "But you'd better have your ass back in the office . . . Say, what the hell is Grace wearing? Is that her *leg?* She wasn't wearing that

153

little number when she came in this morning. What the hell's going on here?"

"Jack, go give yourself an enema. You don't look well at all."

He followed Grace down the escalator.

Fifteen

There are probably eighty or ninety bars between Tenth Street and Canal, but Maddy had managed to find a new one on West Broadway that enlivened the pre-happy hour doldrums with free hors d'oeuvres, delicate wedges of paté on crisp French bread. She picked up two of them from the plate before her, put one, the larger, into her own mouth and the other into the mouth of Neil Astrakhan.

"Feeding ritual," she explained.

"Very colorful," he said. "Of your own devising?"

"Yup."

"And what does it achieve?"

"If I got it right, which is doubtful, the lights go off again all over this burg."

"In the middle of the afternoon? Maddy, you're crude but effective," he said, helping himself to another slice. He did not put one into her mouth.

"So are you," she said. "Give me a break, Neil."

"All right" he said, glancing at his watch. "What is this all about? And make it fast. I have a patient at three-thirty."

"Catherine Donovan."

"What about her?"

"A friend of ours, a friend of mine actually, who knows Catherine, saw her cruising outside Grand Central."

"What do you mean 'cruising'?"

"Cruising. Cruising! What do you think I mean? She had her tits hanging out of her blouse and her skirt hitched up to her belly button and she was with a black whore you could have eaten with a fork."

He rolled the ice around in his scotch.

"Is she sure it was Catherine?"

"It's a he and so he took a *very* good look. It was our Catherine all right."

"Christ," he muttered under his breath.

"Exactly," Maddy replied. She signalled for two more drinks. And more hors d'oeuvres. "Don't tell me this has taken you by surprise, doctor."

"A little. She's on about three different tracks, all running at different speeds. It's hard to keep up."

"Well, she's in the fast lane now."

They sat staring out the window onto West Broadway.

"She thinks you want her husband," he said suddenly. "Do you?"

"You ever think of shaving off your moustache? It would make you look more mature," she said tilting her head appraisingly to one side. "Yes, I think so."

"Maddy."

"Yes and no. How do I know? Tom and I screw, but that's not exactly wanting her husband. He's got to screw somebody, right? So why not me? I'm fresh and young and available." She looked morosely down into her drink. "Neil, this whole thing stinks, really stinks. What's she doing?"

156

"No more about Catherine Donovan. Drink your drink, Maddy. I've got to go."

"Am I crazy or did the lights go out in here?" she said.

While her doctor and her friend sat discussing her condition over drinks and paté, Catherine Donovan was more constructively engaged in running off a hundred copies of a lugubrious report on Bulgarian workers' organizations in the duplicating room of the International Research Council. Making copies of documents in that windowless cell was a task she enjoyed because it took her away from the stares and glares of the corridor outside and gave her a chance to think. And sometimes, while the machine carried on its mindless task of duplicating and collating she would cross the hall and go into the Council library. It was usually empty, as it was today, except when the program officers had their private drinks there late in the afternoon, and so she could sit in one of the deep leather chairs behind the stacks and be at peace.

She was sitting there now, her legs negligently crossed, her white fingers caressing her long black hair, when Mr. Hopper came around the corner of the stacks.

"Oh, hello, Catherine. I didn't know you were in here."

Mr. Hopper, she knew, kept her under constant and unremitting surveillance.

She did not move, as she certainly would have under other circumstances. She sat, still negligent of her dress and legs, still fingering her long black hair. Nor did he. George Hopper held his ground and kept his eyes fixed steadily and brightly on the upper thighs of Catherine Donovan.

"Catherine, baby," he said, "I've got a little piece of friendly advice for you."

"And what would that be?" she said flatly.

"The lunch hours, girlie. They're getting longer and Gene's nose is getting a little out of joint, you know. He's mentioned it to a couple of people."

"He hasn't mentioned it to me."

"That's because you've got old Gene Gillespie hornswoggled, Catherine baby, like almost everybody else around here. You got something on him?"

His fixed smile was beginning to tighten into something else.

"Don't call me baby. I don't like it."

"What are you up to on those lunch hours? Doing something naughty?"

"Very naughty," she said with a smile of her own.

His smile had now totally disappeared. He took an uncertain step toward her.

"Don't move, George. Stay right there."

She uncrossed her legs, put both feet on the ground and began slowly to rock her knees back and forth, in and out.

"Tell me," she said, "what do you figure the odds are that I'm not wearing anything under this skirt?"

"I don't know," he managed to get out between shallow breaths. "Fifty-fifty?"

"Would you pay two hundred to find out?"

There was a long silence in the Council library. George Hopper's eyes remained on her knees, the insides of her thighs. He could see the tops of stocking, a glimpse of the flesh beyond.

"I might," he said at last.

"I thought you might. It's three-thirty now. I'm going out to do some shopping. I'll be back in an hour to say my goodbye to Mr. Gillespie. If there's two hundred dollars on my desk at four-thirty, you get to find out."

She got up from her chair.

"Oh, and tell Astrid to pick up the Xerox copies when they're finished and give them to Gillespie."

At four-thirty an envelope was on her desk. She carefully tore it open. Inside were ten twenty-dollar bills, each of them still smelling of the Citibank machine downstairs on the corner. She picked up her handbag, put the bills in it and walked slowly around the corner to George Hopper's office. Astrid was typing as her station outside.

"Astrid, Gillespie wants to see you right away."

Catherine went past Astrid into the office and closed the door behind her. George Hopper looked up startled from his desk.

"You're really a sporting man, George. And this is your lucky Monday. No panties. See, here's the proof."

She opened her handbag, took out her white cotton panties and threw them on the desk.

"Let me see," he said in a low voice. "Let me see you."

"Seeing costs extra, George. Isn't it worth two hundred just to know? Use your imagination, baby. Use your imagination," she said and left.

George Hopper picked up the panties from the desk, pressed them briefly to his face and placed them in his desk drawer, which he locked.

Catherine went around the corner, passed the darkly scowling Astrid in the corridor and went to the doorway of Mr. Gillespie's office.

"Mr. Gillespie?"

Mr. Gillespie popped to immediate and complete attention.

"Yes, Catherine?"

"Mr. Gillespie, I've been taking a little longer on my lunch hours and I thought I should mention it to you. I've been doing some research. I hope you don't mind and it hasn't inconvenienced you."

"No, of course not, Catherine. You take as long as you need. I'll do just fine."

"Thank you, Mr. Gillespie. I'll make it up to you someday, I promise," she said quietly.

Later, on West Tenth Street Neil Astrakhan gave Catherine as close a look as Eugene Gillespie had. He was searching for some visible clue, but there was none. Catherine Donovan appeared exactly as she had when she first entered his office many months ago. Same clothes, same makeup. Not even the nipples after that one time.

"Catherine, how are you feeling?"

"Fine. Why do you ask? Do I look funny?"

"No, you look fine. Maybe a little tired. Been working hard?"

"Well, I've been looking around for a second job. To support this expensive habit I've acquired."

"What habit?"

"Analysis. What did you think?"

"You know, I was up around Grand Central last week," he lied, "and I thought I saw you on the street. At least it looked like you."

"Was I with a black girl?"

"Yes, I think so."

"That was me. Probably looking for work."

She lay on the couch, arranged her skirt demurely around her knees.

"What kind of work are you looking for?"

"Oh, something creative."

"You're playing with me, Catherine," he said.

"Don't you wish, Neil."

"You've never called me that before."

"It's your name, isn't it. Words don't kill. I'm getting better, you see. Listen. George, Gene, Neil, whore, cunt, hard-on, fuck, clap, ballbuster. How's that?"

"A nice sequence," he said. "The others I recognize but who's George and Gene?"

"Mr. Hopper and Mr. Gillespie. At the Council."

"Well, you haven't whored-cunt-fucked-and-clapped Neil yet. How about George and Gene?"

"Don't be crude, Neil," she said. "Give me a cigarette."

He went over, put a cigarette between her lips and lit it.

160

He looked down quickly into her face. Her eyes were closed, her features calm. He resumed his place in the armchair.

"You started talking about sex the first minute I walked into this office and you still are," she complained. "Don't you have anything else on your mind?"

"It's your mind and that's in analysis, not mine."

"That must make you feel good. The power. Do you think you have control over me, doctor?"

"No," he said. "Do you feel you can control me?"

"Sure," she said simply.

"How?"

"Back to your favorite subject again, doctor?"

Her eyes were still closed.

I told Marvina right away I didn't like his looks, but she has no sense at all in her head. "Go ahead, lady," she said, "he'll cook up fine." Sure. So I backed off in a dark hallway, stupid me, and I lifted my skirt and said, "OK, man, here it is. You can look and you can smell, but *don't touch*. He knelt down all right but then he got that funny glazed look in his eyes and he reached out his filthy hands and grabs my legs. What could I do? I just got him right in the face with my knee. Bash. I think I broke his nose. Two hundred dollars to get his nose broken. Next time *I'll* pick him.

Too bad about Daisy. She got scared and cut out. Nice girl, Daisy, but a little too nervous. It was like I was her daughter or something. Don't do this. Don't do that. Be careful, Catherine. It's not as if I was still twelve years old. God, *that* was a scene. You'd think I'd run off with my old man. Just a little clean fun below decks. My God, four of them. I must have been exhausted. She was the slut, not me, no matter what she said. Now, Catherine, do what mommy tells you. As if I didn't know what was going on in that house. All day long, every day. She must have been taking on half of Bayside. Filthy pigs, all of them.

She turned her head on the couch and looked up at him.

161

"Doctor Astrakhan, if you ever so much as touch me, you know what I'll do."

"Don't worry, Catherine. I won't touch."

She sat up and faced him.

"All right, if you promise. You got two hundred?"

He took out his wallet and extracted two hundred-dollar bills which he put on the table between the couch and the armchair.

She sat and stared at the money without expression. Finally she took the bills and put them in her purse. Without looking at him she walked to the other end of the room and stood facing him.

"Close enough?"

He said nothing.

She came halfway across the room toward him.

"Better?"

He still said nothing.

She moved much closer this time, about three feet from where he was sitting smoking, and slowly raised her skirt. She slid it up over her hips. There was nothing underneath.

Catherine Donovan stood there motionless for half a minute, her dark eyes on him, his on her, without a word or gesture. Then she lowered her skirt, picked up her handbag and left the office. Outside she stood on the landing of the fire stairs for a minute, leaning against the wall, waiting for her knees to steady and her heart to quiet. Then she continued down and out through the lobby to Tenth Street. She turned onto Sixth Avenue and north to Pleasures.

"Dean?"

The young man looked up from his book.

"Is Bill here?"

He looked quickly back to his reading.

"Didn't you hear?" he said. "He was killed last week."

162

She stood there a while.

"Do you mind if I go in the back for a minute?"

"Suit yourself," he said without looking up again.

The room was unchanged. She looked around and under the desk. The black leather case was in one of the drawers. She took it out, placed it on top of the desk and opened it. Empty.

There was a business card on top of the desk. "William Mariner," it said. "Attorney. 62 Horatio Street."

Mariner, she thought. How very fitting.

There weren't four of them; there were five counting Gerald. Big tall good-looking terrible Gerald. Did he start it? Was it his idea in the beginning, luring her onto the *Stella Maris*, like a baby with milk and crackers? She felt sick.

"Don't be afraid, Catherine."

"I'm not afraid. I'm sick."

"Why don't you go below and lie down?"

"Below? I didn't know there was anything downstairs."

They laughed at her, all of them.

"Sure, it's like a regular little house down there. A kitchen and a toilet and beds and everything."

"A toilet?"

"Yeah, it's terrific. Just like a doll's house. Go down and take a look."

She let go of the mast and went unsteadily down the three polished wooden steps behind Gerald.

"See, we told you." They were all five crammed in there, bodies touching. "And here's the can. Want to throw up or something?"

They opened a door for her.

"And here's the beds. Go ahead. Try it."

One hand on her stomach, she lurched toward the bunk, climbed up and sat down on the edge.

"This is sort of nice," she said. "Very cozy."

163

"Go ahead, lie down. You'll feel better."

She put her head on the pillow. If she turned her head to the left she could see the sky through the tiny porthole.

"Don't hang out in here," Dean said through the curtained doorway behind her. "Something bad's going down. Go, please."

She went out into the store, the card clutched in her hand.

She turned back to Dean. He was still standing by the curtained doorway.

"I hate this place," she said. "I'm glad he was killed."

Sixteen

"This one's for you. From the Council."

Tom flipped the letter across the kitchen table to Catherine.

"Your typical non-profit enterprise," he said. "Why didn't they just hand it to you at work and save the postage?"

She opened the envelope. She could see it was a check. She pulled it halfway out. $200.00. Below it was signed "George M. Hopper."

"What is it?" Tom asked.

"A kind of bonus."

She put the envelope into her handbag.

"Well, it all counts," he said. "Why don't you get yourself some new clothes?"

He suddenly remembered about the Israeli.

"Do you and Maddy still go up to that store near Bloomingdale's?"

"Sometimes," she said. "Maddy's not around much these days, is she?"

"Well, she's your friend after all," he said and immediately wished he hadn't. "I don't see her much either. I wonder if she's angry."

"At who?"

He let it go. It would lead nowhere.

"By the way, what ever happened to your friend Daisy? Was that her name?"

"Yes, Daisy. I guess we didn't have much in common."

"You never did tell me what she did. You said she worked near you."

"She's a whore."

"What?"

"A whore. She works Forty-sixth Street. You should try her sometime. She's very sweet and she needs the money. And this is the best part: she looks just like me."

Thomas Donovan looked at his wife to see if she was kidding. Catherine was running her finger around the edge of the table. He couldn't see her eyes but he knew there was no laughter in them.

"What were you doing with a whore? You couldn't even say the word once."

"We were friends, that's all."

"My God!"

"Tom, don't be so self-righteous," she said, looking up from the table. "And they lead lousy lives."

"That I know. What are you doing, conducting a study?"

She was working on the edge of the table again.

"Who was that check from?" he suddenly asked.

"Somebody at the office."

"And what exactly was it for?"

"I don't know. I'm sure he'll tell me."

"Good Christ! What are you up to, Catherine? Does Astrakhan know about any of this?"

166

"Yes."

"Well, that's something."

He reached out and took her hand. She pulled it sharply away.

"Don't touch me, Tom. Please."

"So much for the whore research," he said wearily.

"Tom, I'm just very upset, that's all. I'm having all sorts of dreams and sometimes I can't tell if I'm asleep or awake. Do you ever have dreams like that?"

"Sometimes. Rarely. But they're really knockouts when they happen, I know. It's probably the analysis, all the turning over of the buried past. Do you ever talk about when you were a child?"

"Hardly ever."

"I thought they always try to make you do that," he said.

"I guess I'm not a very apt subject. He says I have a lot of resistance."

"Tell him if he wants I'll send him the book on that. Did you tell him about Daisy?"

"I'm not sure."

He thought she meant she didn't remember.

"Are you going to spend the money?"

"What money?"

"The check, the one you just got. How much was it for?"

"Two hundred."

"Well, I wouldn't be too quick to spend it before I found out what it was for."

Catherine found out what it was for early the next day. At five minutes after nine George Hopper was posted at the side of her desk.

"Get my deposit?" he smiled.

"Yes, I got your check."

She took it out of her handbag and tore it into tiny pieces as he stood watching.

"Why did you do that?" he asked angrily. "You squeezed

167

the hell out of me the other day and here I give you a goodwill advance and you throw it in my face." He lowered his voice and bent over her. "Well, baby, I don't work that way. I'll go along a little bit, but I won't be played for a fool by some two-bit cunt who's so fuckin' hot to trot that she can't keep her bloomers on."

"I told you not to call me baby. I don't like it," she said calmly.

"I don't give a fuck what you like, sweetheart," he said and walked down the corridor and around the corner.

No big deal, Catherine thought. I'll put the hook back into his mouth whenever I choose. She returned content to her work.

At three o'clock the big fish swam upstream and tried to re-insert the hook into his own gaping mouth. Or rather, he sent one of his minnows.

"Mr. Hopper would like to see you in his office, Catherine," Astrid said sweetly. "Right away."

Mr. Hopper had said no such thing, of course. The delicacy of the negotiation precluded anything so crude as "right away." It was Astrid's postscript for her own satisfaction. Catherine pushed her chair back from her desk and followed in Astrid's langorous wake to the Council's Middle East command post.

"Sit down please, won't you, Catherine."

She sat in his armchair, legs neatly and decisively crossed. No open invitation this time, he knew.

George Hopper rose from his desk, went behind his seated guest and closed the office door. Astrid would have to give this one a pass.

"I feel I was terribly rude before and I wanted to apologize," he began, all benign intention. "I would have come to you, but what I wanted to say was private and so I thought it would be better to ask you to come here. Do you understand?"

Catherine understood everything.

"Do you have a cigarette?" was her only response.

George Hopper got up once again, and oozing reconciliation, he carried the cigarettes around to Mrs. Donovan in person. He lit one for her and then, instead of returning to his chair behind the desk, he seated himself familiarly on the corner of the desk next to her.

"As for the *casus belli*, so to speak, I shouldn't have sent you the check in the first place. It was presumptuous and provocative on my part, I know, and for that I apologize as well. Am I forgiven?"

She sat smoking and calculated her own schedule.

"Am I?" he asked again.

"Of course, George. I'm not one to hold a grudge."

It was his turn to lapse into silence. He had simply come back into the water. The hook, still dangling in her hands, was not yet in his mouth. He would have preferred she snap it through his greedy jaws, but if she wouldn't oblige him, then he would have to do it for and to himself.

"Then are we still in business?" he wanted to know.

"Business? What business?"

She jerked it out of his reach. He would have to swim a while longer.

"Our little transaction, Catherine. The one that unfortunate check was intended for."

"You mean, George, that you're willing to lay down two hundred dollars, just to *look* at a mere secretary's pussy? A man like you? You're well educated and intelligent, with a respected position; you can probably have any woman you want."

Catherine Donovan, he thought, you are one mean bitch. That's what he was thinking, but his eyes were upon her hand which lay white and enticing on her lap and which had slowly begun to move to and fro across the smooth fabric of her skirt.

"You could even have a first class whore for two hundred," she continued. "Wouldn't you rather have a professional?"

"I want you," he said softly.

"You still don't understand, do you George?" she smiled. "You don't *get* me at all. You look, that's it." She got up, went over to the window and sat on the sill. Her thighs were now straining in bold outline against her skirt. "And no, George, there's no escalator clause. There's nothing beyond looking, not for you, not for anybody, not for any amount of money. Two hundred to look and no options."

"I'll pay," he pleaded. "You've seen my money already. Catherine, you know I'll pay."

George Hopper was beginning to perspire in the air-conditioned room.

"You mean you don't want a whore?" she asked.

"I don't want a whore. I want you."

"I want you too, George," she said almost gently. "And I am a whore."

"Please don't say that," he said. "It makes me very uncomfortable."

"Have you ever had a whore, George?"

"No," he said in a low voice. "Please."

The plea was undefined, metaphysical. It was a cry for clemency on whatever level she might choose to grant it. But not to remove the hook from his mouth. Not that.

She went behind his desk and sat in George Hopper's leather swivel chair.

"I tell you what," she said with a bright new gleam in her eye. "Bring your two hundred in cash to the main promenade of the Port Authority Bus Terminal this evening at six-thirty and we'll see if we can take care of your special needs."

"The Port Authority? For God's sake, why there of all places? What's wrong with the library here? There's nobody around after five. Or my apartment?"

"Georgie, believe me, it's no fun in private. The danger adds flavor; that's what makes it good. You're too insulated in this office. Don't you want to see how the rest of the world gets it?"

"No, not really. Please, I don't want to go there. It's degrading."

170

"Yes, that's the word I was looking for," she said. "Degrading, exactly. See you at six-thirty, Georgie. Under the clock, as they say. And this is your last shot, so don't blow it again."

She walked over to the door. Her hand rested on the knob as she turned back to him.

"You know, don't you, that Astrid would be only too happy to let you *eat* it, and for *nothing*."

Catherine opened the office door. The generous Astrid was standing there, a sheaf of papers hanging limply from her hand.

"But that's giving it away and that's no fun, is it, George?"

Astrid's gaze followed Catherine Donovan all the way down the hall, and when Catherine was out of sight, she turned her alarmed attention to George Hopper, still seated somewhat uncertainly on the corner of his desk.

"Mr. Hopper, are you all right? Is there anything I can do for you?"

A small smile crept over George Hopper's flushed moist face. Poor Astrid, he thought without sympathy. Poor virtuous Astrid.

At five-fifteen Catherine found Marvina standing glumly at Forty-third and Third.

"Marvina," she cried delightedly, "I've got a real jitterbug this time. Some guy where I work. One of the bosses."

Marvina's naturally optimistic disposition came cheerfully to life.

"Oh, wow! And he's dropping two of them on you?"

"Two of them twice," Catherine explained. "This is the second time around. The first time he paid two bills for a pair of lollipop panties."

"Now that's a spender. My kind of guy," Marvina chuckled. "You just send him around to me when you're finished with him and I'll give him some straight sex, just for variety, you know. If he's got any green left, that is." She scanned the street. "Man, it is bad out here today. There must be a new VD campaign or somethin'. Nothin' is movin'. Nothin'."

171

"Marvina, I want you to come over to the Port Authority with me. I want you to see this one go down."

Marvina looked up and down Forty-third Street.

"OK, sporty, but we split. Can't be workin' for nothin'."

"Deal. Six-thirty in the promenade. You ever work the PA?"

"Honey, we've all worked the PA. I used to have a real cute deal goin' in the Nedick's there till I gave some mick cop a lot too much lip. 'Baby,' he said—I can't do an Irish accent nohow—'baby, you can haul your black ass out of here 'cause you're off the orange juice forever.' And the funny thing was, I really loved the fuckin' stuff, the orange juice I mean. Probably bad for your teeth anyway."

Marvina flashed her still perfect teeth to confirm her theory.

"Come on, O.J.," Catherine urged. "I've still got to change."

At six o'clock Grace was in her personally endowed chair in Thomas Donovan's office, a seat she was occupying with increasing frequency these days. Her tenure had not gone unnoticed, of course, and even Jack Charbonneau, a solitary man not much given to expressing opinions, had one on the subject of Grace Ortega. "Look," he told his audience in the cafeteria, "there's some good in everybody," leaving his listeners to wonder whether he was casting a vote for Puerto Rican statehood or against marital fidelity. Tom was beyond caring in any event, and Grace had never cared in the first place.

"Tom," she said, "in your church can you get a divorce?"

"What do you mean, in *my* church? What are you, a Hindu?"

"Well, it doesn't seem to work the same way everywhere. Can you?" she persisted.

"Are you telling me I should or asking me if I will?"

"Nothing. Forget it," she pouted. "Tomas, sometimes you're very mean."

172

"Want to go to a movie? Look, Grace, I'm sorry." He took her hand. "You know, sometimes I feel very guilty about you."

"Because you sleep with me?"

"Because you deserve something better. I know nice people and pleasant people and smart people. You're all of those things but you're probably the only really good person I know."

"Tomas, don't say that. You're good."

"Grace," he said standing and stretching, "what you don't understand is that in my church you can't be good. Let's go. I'll buy you dinner."

They passed out through the empty offices, across the arcade now crowded with commuters and down the escalator to the promenade.

"Tomas!" she exclaimed, grasping his arm. "You know who I just saw? The whore who chased me off the arcade."

"Don't worry, Gracie dear, I'll protect you." He put his arm around her shoulder. "There isn't a whore in this whole big city that I can't take."

George Hopper made promptness a habit, almost an obsession, so why shouldn't he have been early for his own undoing? He stood uneasily out in the center of the Port Authority promenade and for fifteen minutes fought off public invitations to save his soul, cloud or clear his mind, join the Armed Forces or enter Brigham Young University, raise his consciousness, his blood pressure, his income. In this city it is dangerous, he thought, to stand in any one place for longer than thirty seconds.

"Waiting long?"

Marvina he simply could not look at, except in the eyes of passers-by, where she was amply and stunningly reflected through a haze of wide-eyed blinks and stares. Nor was it altogether easy to take in this new version of Catherine Donovan, the former Ice Maiden who worked in his office. Deeply outlined eyes leaped out of her pale face. The inviting red lips, the threatening red nails. He saw her unrestrained breasts flowing suggestively under her blouse, the curve of her thigh exposed to its top and beyond, the fabric of her skirt stretched taut across the flesh of her groin.

"George, this is Marvina," Catherine said pleasantly, as if she were presiding at tea and introducing the dean's wife. "She's a friend of mine."

George Hopper did not have a B.A. from Haverford and an M. Div. from Yale for nothing. He courteously extended his hand to the attractive lady whose skirt and blouse and curious boots were already beginning to draw a crowd in the promenade.

"Pleased to meet you," he said. It was, he knew immediately, the most stupid thing he had ever said in his life.

"Marvina will take the money, if you don't mind," Catherine said.

George put his hand slowly inside his jacket pocket. This was, he well knew, the final fail-safe, his last chance to spit out that shiny hook and swim safely downstream to a shower, a drink, a peaceful evening alone at home. He withdrew his empty hand.

"Catherine, what is this? What are you doing? Are you punishing me for something I did? If you are, I wish you would tell me what it is. You have me standing here and being smirked at in a public place with you looking like a tart and this person you call your friend who probably is a tart. And you're making me pay for the privilege. Why?"

She drew a little closer to him.

"Because, George, I think sex is something that should blow your head off, and so do you or you wouldn't be standing here with me. Anybody can get laid, but I am going to give you what only a few people can have. George, you'll remember this hard-on for the rest of your boring life." She took Marvina by the hand and drew her closer. "I could draw you a picture, George, but I'm getting very impatient and a little angry, so please give the money to this nice lady so we can get on with it."

174

George Hopper took an envelope from his inside pocket and handed it to Marvina.

"Count it, Marvina," Catherine commanded.

"For Christ sake," George groaned.

Marvina nodded and Catherine took George Hopper by the hand like a child down the same deserted corridor where she had received her own initiation, except it was now an excited Marvina and not a nervous and apprehensive Daisy who followed.

Catherine Donovan stood in the alcove with her back to the wall. George stood before her, already trembling with fear and desire, and Marvina behind him.

"Kneel down," Catherine said.

He stood there paralyzed. Catherine pressed down on his shoulders until at last he knelt directly facing her like a communicant in some strange rite.

"I'm warning you, George" she whispered to the top of the bowed head before her, "it's all wet."

George was now visibly shaking. Marvina moistened her dry lips with her tongue. She too could feel a trembling.

"And do not touch. Do you understand?"

He nodded.

Catherine placed her hands on her hips, took her skirt in her fingers and raised it slowly, over her knees, over her thighs, up to the level of her hips.

George turned slightly away. Marvina grasped his head between her hands and turned it straight ahead, where it remained without constraint.

Fifteen seconds. Thirty seconds.

Catherine had her eyes on Marvina's face behind and above the kneeling George Hopper. She was watching the expression there, the excitement shining in Marvina's eyes, the tension in her pulsing mouth and jaw.

Suddenly George Hopper lunged forward with a soft, almost inaudible cry. His hands seized Catherine's hips and he buried his face deep into the glistening place forbidden by Catherine Donovan to all men.

The breath went with a rush out of her throat. Her head tossed wildly from side to side as George Hopper fed hungrily upon her. Marvina heard her gasp, looked up, saw her contorted face and fiercely tossing hair. "Jesus Christ!" she exclaimed and tried to grasp George by his shoulders and neck. She could not dislodge him. Marvina seized him by his hair, dug her long fingernails into his scalp and finally tore him away from Catherine. He fell backward onto the pavement. Catherine still stood where she was, her body vibrating in great spasms against the wall, her head thrown dizzily back, her eyes closed.

"Honey, stop!"

Marvina clasped her in her arms and held her tightly to herself. She brought her face close to Catherine's own. "Stop," she pleaded. "Stop, it's over."

Gradually the shaking diminished, then ended. Catherine slowly opened her eyes. She was still in Marvina's arms.

"Where is he?" Catherine asked softly.

"He's gone," Marvina whispered. "It's all right. He's gone."

"I'll kill him," Catherine said. "I am going to kill him."

Seventeen

She was sitting in the living room calmly reading a magazine when the phone rang a little later that same evening.

"Catherine? Hi, I'm calling from the office. Something has come up. I'm going to be a little late."

She curled the phone cord tightly around her finger.

"No, Tom."

"No what? I've got things I have to take care of here."

"No, not tonight. Send her home, whoever she is. I want you here. And right away, Tom. You understand?"

"Catherine, is anything the matter?"

"No, nothing at all. Just send her away and come home."

She hung up and went back to her magazine.

Tom returned slowly to the table where he and Grace had been having their espresso. He signalled for the check.

"Tomas," Grace said, "sometimes I feel guilty too. Like I'm stealing."

"Stealing me?"

"Yes, stealing you from your wife."

He paid the check and sat there with the wallet still in his hand.

"It may not matter," he said. "You may just be doing salvage."

"What's salvage?" she wanted to know.

"When a crew abandons a ship, by rights it belongs to anybody who gets there and throws a tow-line on it. I have to go."

"I thought we were going to the movies?"

"Not tonight, Grace. There's been a change in course. Stormy weather ahead."

"Tomas, what are you talking about? Is anything wrong?"

"We'll soon see," he said. He took a ten dollar bill from his wallet and slid it across the table to Grace. "Here, take a cab home please. I don't want you on the subway."

"Tomas, if anything is the matter, you promise you'll call me?"

"Yes, I'll call you."

He put her in a cab and found one for himself.

Catherine was still reading her magazine when he came in. He saw her under the light slowly turning the pages with bright lacquered nails. It was the nails he noticed first, lit from above in her bright pool of light. Then, when she raised her face to his, he saw the crimson lips, the dark theatrical eyes. The dress. The shoes.

He sat in the armchair facing her.

"Where?" he asked.

"It doesn't matter," she said.

She closed the magazine and let it slide to the floor.

Would he, he wondered. If he were crossing the arcade of the PA and saw her sitting where Grace was that day, Would he stop and look? Would he approach her, engage in negotiations.

He had never done that with anyone. Could he do it with his wife?

She took a cigarette from her handbag and lit it.

"Tom, I think I need a drink."

He went into the kitchen, opened the refrigerator and looked in.

"Wine or vodka?" he called back into the living room.

"Vodka," she said. "Just ice."

He brought two of them back to the living room.

"I guess I'll just have to get used to having lipstick on the booze glasses," he smiled.

"Tom, don't start getting off on this, please." She sipped her drink. "It has nothing to do with you. It never has."

"Maybe not," he said, "but for better or worse, we're married. I am your husband after all."

"No, you're not," she said quietly. "In one way you are, yes, and I'm grateful to you for that. I don't know what your reasons were, but there aren't many men who would have put up with me."

"It wasn't so hard."

"I'm not talking about the sex," she said. "You can beg, borrow or steal that. Especially when you have a terrible, misunderstanding wife, women get all juicy with sympathy."

"I never said that about you," he protested. "I never claimed sympathy."

"Maddy told me once you were a real gentleman," she smiled. "I guess that's what she must have meant, that you never claimed sympathy. Did you ever feel abused?"

"No," he said. "Never."

"Then maybe I shouldn't feel so sorry for you."

Her drink hung limply, knowingly in one hand, a cigarette in the other, and her long black hair descended about her shoulders, onto those breasts already half visible under her open blouse. How did he do it, he wondered. How did he live for more than three years, sleep every night in the same bedroom with the explosively sexual woman who was sitting under the reading lamp opposite him? He wanted her. Even now.

"You shouldn't have let me, Tom, not for my sake but for yours. You should have made me put out or get out. Were you passive with the others too?"

He did not respond. He hadn't answered his own question yet.

"No," she continued. "No need. You just jerked them around a little and they popped. Little pops." She drank. "And then you came home and sat here and waited for the big boom. Which never came."

"I'll pay you, Catherine."

She smiled.

"You're sitting there, aren't you, waiting for me to say, 'Oh no, Tom. For you it's free. After all, you're family.' Is that it?"

"No, I'd pay."

"You've already had better for nothing," she said.

"No, I haven't."

"No, Tom, I don't mean with them. I mean with me. The first time. Nobody's bought that yet. And you got it for nothing."

"Maybe that's what I've been paying off over the last three years."

"No you haven't, you clever conniving bastard." There was no anger in her voice. "You've been making down payments on the next one."

She held out her glass to him.

He got them both another drink.

"What are you going to do?" he asked.

"What do you mean? Nothing. I'm going to do nothing. You're going to move out."

Why wasn't he shocked by that casual command? Or at least startled?

180

"Just like that," he said. "What about all those down payments?"

"Speculators get burned sometimes," she shrugged. "What can I tell you?"

He looked at her and he wanted her. Like the first time. In these same clothes.

"Catherine, I want you."

The frown was gradual, like a distant storm approaching a picture landscape. It deepened, grew dark across her painted face.

"Tom, if you touch me, I'll kill you, too."

"Me, too?" his voice was even but the drink was trembling in his hand. He could feel the old fear, the always repressed but always present fear he felt of his incalculable wife. "Catherine, what have you done?"

"Nothing," she said. "I'm just warning you."

They sat and drank in silence. He was still frightened and his fear had destroyed his desire. Forever, he hoped. His only thought now was to be out of there, away from what seemed to him her increasingly dangerous presence.

"I'll be gone in the morning," he said.

"No," she said simply. "Tonight. Maddy or somebody will take you in, I'm sure. You can pick up the rest of your stuff later."

Yes, he thought, tonight. Someplace else, someplace safer than Catherine O'Rourke's bedroom.

She put her drink on the table and got up.

"I'm going out for a while," she said. "So you can make your phone calls."

She extended her hand. It was hot to his touch. For the first time.

"Goodbye, Tom."

She walked up Lexington Avenue, her hips swinging slowly and her eyes boldly upon the faces approaching her. Without fear. At the corner of Thirty-second she stopped and brought a newspaper, scanned the headlines. She heard the familiar noises beginning somewhere behind her.

She looked up at the man who had sold her the newspaper. His eyes rested boldly on her half-exposed breasts.

"You got a lousy neighborhood here, Jack," she said. "You ever think of relocating to Westchester?"

"What, and miss you, sweetie? You're worth the price of admission."

"The price of admission," she smiled, "is two hundred balloons. And that's just the previews. So save your pennies, friend."

Catherine Donovan gave her husband an hour, for her an hour of idle cruising, a plain joyride of the type neither the anxious Marvina nor the business-like Daisy would have understood, she reflected. Staking out the territory, inspecting the plantation, visiting with the hired hands. The joy of ownership.

When she returned Tom had gone from her life, if he had ever been there.

Catherine was carefully not there when Tom cleared out the rest of his possessions, nor did she return immediately to work. She called and cashed in seven of the scores of memorial, religious, personal and sick days she had accumulated at the International Research Council. She used the time to rearrange the apartment to her own liking, which include getting rid of their twin beds in favor of a foam and down arena the size and shape of a hockey rink, which she trimmed with ribbons and lace. She replaced the discount house brand vodka with Stolichnaya.

The Monday after Tom's departure Catherine sat down and wrote a letter to George Hopper.

Dear George;

I hope you will accept my apologies for what happened the

other evening. All I can say in my defense is that I've been under considerable personal strain these past months. I've been in the process of separating from my husband and I think it must have been the stress of working that out that caused me to act in the extraordinary way I did toward you.

I cannot hope that you will forgive me since I embarrassed you in public. Maybe it will help for you to know that I embarrassed myself as well. I think I now understand my behavior and perhaps you can understand it as well.

Though I cannot ask your forgiveness, I do ask that you give me another chance. You have always been kind to me at the Council and so I dare hope you will be kind to me again and let me show you that you were not seeing the real Catherine Donovan the other evening.

I will call you in a couple of days at your home, if I may. I will understand perfectly if you hang up and refuse to talk to me. But what I would like, if you will only permit it, is for us to have a quiet dinner together and to try to restore our relationship on a better basis. I like you, George; I think you are a kind and compassionate and attractive man and I mistreated you terribly. Please allow me to take you to dinner. Let me show you a woman you can perhaps learn to like.

Affectionately,
Catherine

She called George Hopper three days later. He would be delighted, he said, to have dinner. No hard feelings. Maybe he had brought it on himself after all. We all have our problems, God knows, even George Hopper. Rich aboriginal Quaker guilt flowed across the phone lines, very finely etched with just a breath of theology from the Yale Divinity School.

Catherine had no intention of revealing her designs to Neil Astrakhan, so the make-up came off, the interesting new skirts, blouses and shoes remained in the closet. Back to basics for the good doctor. Stick to the soft past, not the hard future.

She seated herself in the armchair.

"You're looking well," he began.

"I've had a few days off. It was a nice change."

She watched him studying her. He would find nothing, she knew.

"Catherine, Tom called me. He said that you and he were separated."

"Yes, that's true. It was a friendly parting, I think. I hope. I don't blame Tom for anything."

"Do you blame yourself?"

"No, not at all. It just didn't work out, that's all. Just like my analysis."

Neil Astrakhan sat puffing his cigar.

"I'd like to end," she continued. "To have next week be our final session."

Neither spoke.

"Aren't you going to say anything?" she said at last.

"I do have one question," he said. "I've always wondered what happened to your brother Gerald."

"He fell off the boat. Dead drunk, as usual."

She rested her head back in the armchair.

"Rolled right off, plop, just like that, into Little Neck Bay. Poor Gerald," she sighed.

"Did you see it?"

"Ummm, probably."

"You don't seem to have shed many tears over it."

She opened her eyes again, began collecting her things.

"I was only a child at the time," she said. "Only a baby really. What could I know about it?"

"Before you go, Catherine, I thought you might offer to give me my two hundred dollars back."

"Why?" she smiled. "Did you think we were playing Monopoly?"

184

He shrugged.

"What's the matter?" she pressed. "Don't you think you got your money's worth?"

"Two hundred is pretty steep for a look."

"There have been no complaints so far," she said, inspecting her unpainted fingernails. "Are you registering an official complaint?"

"No, I guess not," he said. "How much to touch?"

She looked up sharply into his face.

"You'll know next time," she said in a voice that cut through the quiet of the office like a knife.

She stood up and offered her hand.

"Well, thank you, Doctor Astrakhan. I hope it was fun for you."

"You sound like you're not coming back," he said. "Didn't you say you wanted one final session next week?"

"Things happen."

"Like walking in front of a car, you mean, or getting struck by a stray meteorite?"

"Something like that," she smiled. "Anyway, I'm at the same address, and if I don't show up you can always bill me there. I always pay my debts."

She went to the door, turned, her hand on the knob.

"I'm very frightened," she said quietly.

He hadn't heard what she said. It was no matter; she was gone.

Eighteen

George Hopper had her buzzed from her lobby on Twenty-ninth Street where he now stood wearing his guilt openly and lacking only a bouquet in his hand to seal an act of perfect contrition for a sin he had never committed. And Catherine Donovan descended fifteen floors wearing a dress and a demeanor so innocent that the elevator doors parted in automatic astonishment.

"Hello, George," she smiled. "I must say you've been very understanding."

"Hey, come on. No more of that. That's over. Let's forget it and enjoy ourselves this one Saturday night like two adults."

An innocuous, open-ended invitation to some simple pleasures between consenting adults. How not?

"And *I* will take *you* to dinner," he huffed.

When George Hopper said he'd do it, he did it, he liked to think, and by God, he did it. He took her to the Russian Tea Room and they had caviar blini and champagne.

"Catherine, when are you coming back to work? We miss you."

"In a couple of days. I just needed a little time to get myself together."

George was of an age and a disposition that did not much fancy girls who said they were getting their thing, their act or their shit together. Getting yourself together was quite another matter, however, especially when you had breasts like Catherine Donovan's.

"I know how it is," George graciously volunteered. "I've been through it myself. Divorces are bad business. It's been five years for me and I'm still a little shaky."

"What were the grounds, George?"

Somehow somebody had taught Catherine Donovan, that ace fireballer, to throw curves, George reflected unhappily.

"Oh, the usual," he said into his blini.

"What's the usual?"

"I guess we each found somebody else along the way."

"And what happened to your 'somebody'?"

"My 'somebody,' " he laughed, "found somebody else. I'm not very interesting. Why don't we talk about you," he suggested.

"No, I think you're very interesting, George. Do you like being a single man in New York?"

"It has its attractions," he said too modestly. "You certainly get to eat out a lot."

"The ladies must love you at their tables," she said shyly, "an interesting, attractive single man."

"You don't have to be interesting," he chuckled. He leaned over the table conspiratorily. "Just heterosexual. That's interesting enough for most ladies. You know there are parts of this city where the species is almost extinct."

"Really?" she gasped.

Did he feel her knee graze his under the table?

"And how. Here's to us, Catherine," he toasted her with his champagne tulip, "the last two straights in New York City."

187

They clinked glasses and drank.

Now it was her turn to explain and entertain, and as she talked George Hopper found himself wishing she had shown a little more imagination in her clothes this pleasant evening. That last outfit wasn't all *that* bad, after all. Not entirely appropriate for the Russian Tea Room perhaps, but it certainly made its point, it did, he smiled to himself. And my God, the body on her.

"Hey, Catherine," he began a trifle hesitantly, "your black friend, she was really a looker under all the crapola."

"She wasn't really my friend, but you're right, George, she's really quite attractive."

"Those teeth are really something. Jesus, imagine. . ." he trailed off into his champagne.

"Did you say something?" Catherine inquired politely.

"No, not so's you'd notice."

"You know," Catherine said, "it's funny about clothes and makeup. Take Marvina. Now there's a really sensational-looking girl who would be absolutely breathtaking without a stitch on her or even any make-up at all. And yet she wears all that stuff to attract men, I guess. But suppose she was in your apartment, George, all alone with you. Would you want her to be with or without the makeup, do you think?"

George thought about it for no more than four seconds.

"With."

"But what does it add?" she wanted to know.

Fantasy, George, fantasy. Go ahead and say it, he urged himself. The same smell of cunt that late had risen from that ripe piece of ass sitting across from you. That was beginning to rise afresh, as urgently as before, from somewhere under the crisp white tablecloth between them.

"I don't know. That's a hard one," is what he actually said.

They finished with a liqueur. And one more toast.

"To a future," he proposed.

"What future, George?"

"Oh, any old future. OK, let's go short-term. To the rest of the evening."

They drank to that.

There was a slight chill in the air on Fifty-seventh Street.

They walked, with a small space between them, up Sixth Avenue to Central Park South.

The moment. The bar at the St. Moritz lay right; his apartment, left.

"In the mood for a quiet evening?" he asked.

"Oh, yes. It's been a very busy day. I had to buy new drapes."

Easy. So easy. He steered her gently left, toward Columbus Circle and Lincoln Center.

George Hopper had a marvelous, twentieth floor view of Lincoln Center Plaza. It glittered in all its flood-lit and fountained splendor far below them.

"Oh George, I love it," she exclaimed out the window to the city below.

"Some wine?"

"Well, maybe a little bit." She turned back to her host. "And real oriental carpets!"

"The colonial loot of the Middle East," he glowed. "A king's ransom in dinars went into those babies."

He went into the kitchen to get their drinks. Catherine kicked off her shoes and slowly inspected the room. Along and between the expensive teak bookcases were hung pictures of tall ships, sleek and slender sailboats with only tanned and handsome men on their gleaming decks. George in his sailing gear looked hardy and clean.

"You know what?" he said from behind her. He held a tray with two wineglasses on it.

"What, George."

"I'd like to take you sailing some time. Have you ever been sailing?"

She sat down on the couch and tucked her legs up beneath her.

Yes, a long time ago on a black, rolling sea, where only garbage and condoms hung motionless around the hull of the *Stella Maris*. Tied spread-eagled on a bunk with my dress riding up over my hips, that's how I sailed, George. With a crew of four drunken teenagers and my brother Gerald charting the course.

"Come on, Catherine, it's just a game. We're like pirates and we've captured you. Yeah, like that. So we've got to tie you up, don't we?"

"Look, she's got flowers on her panties."

"Don't spook the kid, for Christ sake."

"You're really cute, Catherine, and when you grow up I'll bet you'll really be a knockout."

"In three years you'll be givin' all of us a hard-on, won't you, you little cunt."

She heard nothing, said nothing. She was looking at the darkening sky out of the porthole. Holding onto it as if it were her life.

"I wonder what's she's hiding under the flowers?"

They all looked at Gerald O'Rourke. What bearing, captain?

"Why don't we look and see," he said stupidly.

They looked. And they killed her. Many times over. And when they were finished they left two dollars on the pillow next to her head.

"Would you like that?" George Hopper asked again.

"Oh? Sailing? Maybe. Sometime."

"You know, Catherine, you're not at all what you seem."

She slowly raised her eyes to the man sitting opposite her, his gaze stiff and bright, the wine glass slowly twisting in his hands.

"Am I better or worse, do you think?"

Worse he hoped, as bad as that other time, when the pain

190

and the terrifying pleasure of her ran together and shook him where he knelt.

"Oh, better, much better," he smiled. "Some more wine, mate?"

She looked down again at her glass, which was still almost full.

"I don't think so. Not right now."

"Well, I can use a refill I think."

He got up from the sofa beside her and went into the kitchen. He opened the refrigerator and took out an unopened bottle of Pinot Noir from behind the chilled vodka.

I need some more tonic, he noticed. He wrote it down on a shopping list attached to the side of the refrigerator.

"What a lovely kitchen."

He glanced over his shoulder. She was standing smiling in the kitchen doorway, one hip resting comfortably against the jamb while her dark eyes ranged up and around the copper pots and pans suspended from the ceiling. He turned back to the bottle caught between his knee and pulled sharply at the corkscrew.

"I like to cook," he grunted. "Do you?"

She said nothing. She came up behind him as he bent over and thrust his own ten-inch slicing knife deep into his right kidney. He turned, his face amazed, and the bottle slid slowly, still intact, to the floor. A tiny trickle of blood appeared at the corner of his mouth as he crumpled forward, his eyes still on her, and came to rest at her feet.

She removed the knife, carefully washed it in the sink and replaced it in the wooden rack from which she had taken it. She dried her hands and walked around his body back into the living room. She put on her shoes, poured her undrunk wine into his potted spider plant and placed the glass in her purse. Then she let herself out of his apartment and caught a cab near Lincoln Center. It was done.